DOCTOR DOLITTLE'S GARDEN

THE YEARLING DOCTOR DOLITTLE BOOKS

THE STORY OF DOCTOR DOLITTLE
THE VOYAGES OF DOCTOR DOLITTLE
DOCTOR DOLITTLE'S CIRCUS
DOCTOR DOLITTLE'S CARAVAN
DOCTOR DOLITTLE AND THE GREEN CANARY
DOCTOR DOLITTLE'S POST OFFICE
DOCTOR DOLITTLE'S GARDEN
DOCTOR DOLITTLE IN THE MOON

YEARLING BOOKS/YOUNG YEARLINGS/YEARLING CLASSICS are designed especially to entertain and enlighten young people. Charles F. Reasoner, Professor Emeritus of Children's Literature and Reading, New York University, is consultant to this series.

For a complete listing of all Yearling titles,
write to Dell Readers Service,
P.O. Box 1045, South Holland, Illinois 60473.

THE CENTENARY EDITION
A YEARLING BOOK

Published by
Dell Publishing
a division of
The Bantam Doubleday Dell Publishing Group, Inc.
666 Fifth Avenue
New York, New York 10103

ISBN: 0-440-40103-8

Printed in the United States of America

November 1988

10 9 8 7 6 5 4 3 2 1

CW

I would like to acknowledge the following editors whose faith in the literary value of these children's classics was invaluable in the publication of the new editions: Janet Chenery, consulting editor; Olga Fricker, Hugh Lofting's sister-in-law, who worked closely with the author and edited the last four original books; Lori Mack, associate editor at Dell; and Lois Myller, whose special love for Doctor Dolittle helped make this project possible.

CHRISTOPHER LOFTING

· Contents ·

PART THREE

PART FOUR

· Illustrations ·

PART ONE

· The First Chapter ·

THE DOG MUSEUM

I SUPPOSE there is no part of my life with the Doctor that I, Thomas Stubbins, look back on with more pleasure than that period when I was assistant manager of the zoo.

I had joined the Doctor several years ago and had been taught by him and his wonderful old parrot Polynesia to speak a few animal languages too. The regular household now consisted of Dab-Dab the duck, who was the housekeeper, Jip the dog, Too-Too the owl, Gub-Gub the pig, Chee-Chee the monkey, and a few others. The only other human in the house was Bumpo, the African prince whom we had met on our travels, and who now was on an extended leave from his college in England.

We had come to call that part of the Doctor's garden where so many animals now lived together "Animal Town." One of my greatest difficulties was in keeping down the membership in the various clubs. Because of course a limit had to be put on them. The hardest one to keep in check was the Home for Crossbred Dogs. Jip was always trying to sneak in some waif or stray after dark; and I had to be quite stern and hardhearted if I did not want the Mongrels' Club disorganized by overcrowding.

But while the Doctor and I agreed that we must keep a fixed limit on all memberships, we encouraged development, expansion, and new ideas of every kind on the part of the animals themselves that would help to make Animal Town a more comfortable place to live in. Many of these were extremely interesting. Among them was the Dog Museum.

For many years the Doctor had had a museum of his own. This was a large room next to the study where bones, mineral specimens, and other natural-history things were kept. There is an old saying: Imitation is the sincerest form of flattery. A natural interest in bones often led the dogs to contemplate this display and finally to start a museum of their own.

This was helped to some extent by a peculiar dog who had some months before become a member of the club. The peculiarity of his character was that he had an inborn passion for collecting. Prune stones, umbrella handles, doorknobs—there was no end to the variety of his collections. He always maintained that his prune-stone collection was the largest and finest in the country.

This dog's name was Quetch. He was a great friend of Toby's, who had first introduced him and put him up for membership at the club. He was a good second to Toby in upholding the rights of the small dogs at the clubhouse and seeing that they didn't get bullied out of any of their privileges. In fact, Blackie and Grab always said that the small dogs, with Toby and Quetch to champion them, bossed the club a good deal more than they had any business to. Well,

Quetch it was (he was a cross between a West Highland terrier and an Aberdeen) that first suggested the idea that the Mongrels' Club should have a museum of its own. With his passion for collecting, he was probably counting on getting the job of museum curator for himself—which he eventually did.

The House Committee met in solemn council to discuss the pros and cons and ways and means. The idea was finally adopted by a large majority vote, and a section of the gymnasium was screened off to form the first headquarters of the museum.

Quetch (he was always called "Professor" by the other members of the club)—Professor Quetch, besides being a keen scientist, had a genius for organization almost as good as the white mouse's. And even he could not find fault with the general enthusiasm with which the Dog Museum was supported, and contributed to, by the members of the club. There was hardly a dog in the Home who didn't turn to collecting and bringing in material. And Quetch the curator had his paws more than full receiving and arranging the continuous flow of specimens of every kind that poured in.

The museum was not confined to natural history. It was also an archeological or historical museum. The Bones Department was perhaps the largest. Personally, I don't think that any student of comparative anatomy would have found it scientifically very helpful. For the bones were mostly beef, mutton, and ham bones.

But not all. There were fish bones. In fact there was one whole fish that Professor Quetch proudly ordered me to label, *The Oldest Fish in the World.* I could well believe it was. Blackie the retriever had dug it up—from the place

"Professor Quetch"

where someone had carefully buried it a long time ago. Its odor was so far-reaching that the members of the Badgers' Tavern (which was at least a hundred yards away from the Home for Crossbred Dogs) sent in a request that something be done about it. They said that while they were not usually oversensitive to smells, this one kept them awake at night. Professor Quetch was very much annoyed and sent a message back to the badgers that they were a lot of lowbrow, meddlesome busybodies who didn't appreciate science. But some of the Doctor's neighbors across the

"They were seen by the colonel and chased"

street also complained; and the oldest fish in the world had to go—back to the garbage heap.

The archeological side of the Dog Museum was even more varied and extensive than the natural-history departments. Here could be found Quetch's own priceless collection of prune stones, umbrella handles, and doorknobs. But these formed only a small part of the whole. The habit of digging—generally for rats—natural to all dogs, now led to the unearthing of treasures of every variety. Saucepan lids, bent spoons, top hats, horseshoes, tin cans, pieces of iron pipe, broken teapots—there was hardly anything in the way of hardware and domestic furnishings that wasn't represented. A sock that had been worn full of holes by the great Doctor himself was one of the most sacred and important exhibits.

For the first few days there was a general frenzy of digging. Jip and Kling had heard the Doctor say that the Romans had once had a military camp on the site now occupied by the town of Puddleby. They were determined that they'd find Roman jewelry if they only dug patiently enough. Among other places they tried was Colonel Bellowes's tulip bed. They had just dug up a bulb when they were seen by the colonel and chased. But they got away—and home with the bulb. And that was how the Botanical Department of the museum began. The bulb in question had a label set under it reading:

> This orchid was donated by the famous naturalist and explorer, Jip. The intrepid collector was disturbed at his work and chased for miles by savage natives. He eluded his pursuers, however, and succeeded in bringing back this priceless specimen to the Dog Muesum.

· The Second Chapter ·

QUETCH

THE Dog Museum continued for much longer than I had thought it would. My private opinion had been that the dogs were only captivated by the novelty of the idea and would drop it altogether when its newness had worn off. Some weeks after its beginning the collections had grown so vast that they filled the whole gymnasium. During the semifinal bout of a wrestling contest a Great Dane threw Blackie the retriever through the dividing screen and landed him in the middle of the Botanical Department. It was clear that the gymnasium was getting crowded out by the museum.

So a second meeting of the House Committee was called. And it was decided that since athletics were equally important with science, most of the junk should be thrown out, and only those things kept that were really genuine and of special application to dogs and dog history.

Jip's famous golden collar (which he only wore on holidays and occasions of importance) was made one of the star exhibits. There were also a few bones that Professor

"The semifinal bout of a wrestling contest"

Quetch insisted had been chewed by the great dogs of history. There was also a small keg that he said had been carried around the necks of the St. Bernard dogs who went to the aid of lost travelers in the snow-swept passes of the Alps. How he knew the record of these relics no one could tell. On the other hand, no one could deny it when he put up a label under a veal bone saying that this object had been the earliest plaything of the Empress Josephine's pet poodle.

At all events, the enormous array of hardware and rubbish that had formed the first displays gave place to one or two glass cases where a small collection of objects of great virtue was set forth. And for many years these remained a permanent part of the institution and all visitors, whether dogs or people, were shown them. Professor Quetch never allowed visitors into the museum, however, without personally conducting them, to see that they didn't lean on the cases—if they were people—or, if they were dogs, that they didn't take away the historic bones.

Both Toby and Kling had often told me that they knew that Professor Quetch had led rather an interesting life, and I could well believe it, for he was certainly a dog of individuality and character. He was not easy to persuade, however. In spite of his being, like Toby, a self-important, plucky little animal, he wasn't boastful or given to talking about himself. He had always, when asked to tell the story of his life, made the excuse that he was too busy with his duties as curator of the museum.

However, now that the museum had been considerably reduced in size, he did not have to give so much attention to it. And one day Jip came to me highly delighted with the news that Quetch had promised tomorrow night to give us an account of his life, which was to be entitled "The Story of the Dog Who Set Out to Seek His Fortune."

Feeling it would probably be a good yarn well told, I asked the Doctor if he would come and listen. In former times he had frequently attended the dogs' after-supper storytellings. But of late he had seldom had the time to spare. However, he said he would make this a special occasion and be there without fail.

When the following night came the dogs' dining room was jammed. For not only was every single member present, eagerly waiting to hear the yarn, but it turned out that this was Guest Night, the second Friday in the month, when members were allowed to bring friends to dinner as guests of the club.

"I was born," Professor Quetch began, "of poor but honest parents. My father was a hardworking Aberdeen terrier and my mother was a West Highland of excellent pedigree. Our owners were small farmers in Scotland. My father helped regularly with the sheep. In spite of his size, he was a mighty good sheepdog and could round up a flock or cut out a single ewe from the herd with great skill. When we children were puppies we got fed well enough because we were easy to feed, not requiring much more than milk. But as soon as we began to grow up into regular dogs it was another story. We saw then that the farmer that owned us had hardly enough food most of the time to feed his own family and the hands who worked for him, let alone a large litter of hungry terriers.

"We lived in a stable behind the farmhouse, where we had an old disused horse stall to ourselves. It was well lined with dry straw, snug and warm. One night I happened to lie awake late and I overheard my mother and father talking. Their names were Jock and Jenny.

" 'You know, Jock,' said my mother, 'very soon that farmer is going to get rid of these puppies of ours. I heard him talking about it only the other day.'

" 'Well,' said my father, 'I suppose that was to be expected. They'll keep one or two, I imagine. I hope they leave Quetch here. He seems a bright youngster and is already quite a help to me with those silly sheep. For the rest, I think they're rather stupid.'

" 'Stupid, indeed!' snapped my mother with great indig-

"He was a mighty good sheepdog"

nation. 'They're every bit as clever as their father, that's certain.'

" 'All right, have it your own way, Jenny,' said my father, snuggling his nose down into the straw to go to sleep—he never cared for arguments anyway—'have it your own way. But you can hardly expect McPherson to keep the whole litter when he can barely support his own family.'

"With that my father fell asleep and I fell to thinking. First of all, it seemed to me very wrong that dogs should be disposed of in this haphazard, hit-and-miss fashion. If we were given away, to whom would we be given? Had dogs no rights at all? My father was a worker on the farm, doing his daily job as faithfully and as well as any of the clodhoppers who drove the plow or cut the corn. And here he was calmly talking about his own children being given away as though they were apples or turnips! It made me quite angry. I lay awake far into the night wondering why dogs were not allowed to lead their own lives and shape their own careers. It was an outrage. I got myself quite worked up over it. And before I fell asleep I made up my mind that no one was going to give *me* away as though I were no more than an old pair of shoes. I was an individual, the same as the farmer himself. And I was going to make the world acknowledge that fact or know the reason why."

· The Third Chapter ·

THE DICK WHITTINGTON DOG

PERHAPS the only notable thing about this yarn of mine is that it is the story of a dog trying to lead his own life. I know of course that there are many of you present who have struggled to do the same. That was one reason why I wasn't keen to tell a story: I didn't feel that my life had anything particularly thrilling about it. But at all events what small adventures I ran into may have been different from your own, and the way I attacked the problem of winning liberty and independence for myself may interest you.

"A few days after I had overheard my parents' conversation I began to see that my mother's fears were right. Almost every day McPherson, the farmer, would bring friends of his in to see us, hoping they'd be willing to adopt one or other of us. As luck would have it, I was selected the very first. A stupid, fat man—I think he was a farmer too—chose me out of the whole litter. I wouldn't have chosen him from among a million. He had no wits at all and no—er—refinement, none whatever. He turned me over and prodded me and examined me as though I were a pig for the fatting market instead of a dog. I determined right away that whatever happened I wouldn't become *his* property. Luckily he couldn't take me immediately and he asked McPherson to keep me for him a couple of days, at the end of which he would come and fetch me.

"I had heard of boys setting out to seek their fortunes. Never of a dog. And yet why not? The more I thought of the idea, the more it appealed to me. I had to go somewhere if I didn't want to be taken away by that stupid man. I had seen nothing of the world so far. Very well then: I would set out to seek my fortune—yes, tomorrow!

"The next morning I was up before any of the farm was stirring. I had collected several old bones and, with these as all my earthly possessions tied up in a red handkerchief, I set out to carve a career for myself. I remember the morning so well. It was late in the fall and the daylight would not appear for an hour yet. But an old rooster was already crowing in a hoarse voice through the misty chill air as I gained the road and looked back at the farm buildings huddled in the gloom of the hollow. With a light heart I waved my tail at him and trotted off down the road.

"Dear me, how inexperienced I was! I realize that now. Literally I knew nothing—not even the geography of the immediate neighborhood around the farm. I didn't know where the road I was traveling along led to. But at that time such a thing only added to the thrill of the adventure. I would stick to this road, I told myself, and see what fortune it brought me to.

"After I had jogged along for about an hour I began to feel very much like breakfast. I therefore retired off the road into a hedge and opened my bundle of bones. I se-

"I set out to carve a career for myself"

lected a ham bone that had not been quite so thoroughly chewed as the rest and set to work on it. My teeth were young and good and I soon managed to gnaw off the half of it.

"After that I felt much better, though still somewhat hungry. I repacked my baggage, but just as I was about to set off I thought I heard a noise on the other side of the hedge. Very quietly I crept through, thinking I might surprise a rabbit and get a better breakfast. But I found it was only an old tramp waking up in the meadow where, I

"It was only an old tramp waking up"

suppose, he had spent the night. I had a fellow feeling for him. He was homeless too and, like me, a gentleman of the road. Within the thicket I lay and watched him a moment. There was a herd of cows in the field. Presently the tramp went and began milking one of them into a tin that he carried. When he had the tin filled he brought it back to the corner of the field where he had slept and set it down. Then he went away—I suppose to get something else. But while he was gone I crept out of the hedge and drank up all the milk.

"Considerably refreshed, I set off along the road. But I hadn't gone more than a few hundred yards when I thought I'd go back and make the tramp's acquaintance. Maybe I felt sort of guilty about the milk. But anyway a fellow feeling for this adventurer whom I had robbed made me turn back.

"When I regained the corner of the meadow I saw him in the distance milking the cow again. I waited till he returned. Then I came out and showed myself.

" 'Ah, young feller, me lad!' says he. 'So it was you who pinched my milk. Well, no matter. I got some more now. Come here. What's your name?'

"Well, he seemed a decent sort of man and I kind of palled on to him. I was glad of his company. On both sides it seemed to be taken for granted that we would travel together along the road. He was much better at foraging food than I was—in some ways; and I was better than he was in others. At the farmhouses he used to beg meals, which he always shared with me. And I caught rabbits and pheasants for him, which he cooked over a fire by the roadside. Together we managed very well.

"We went through several towns on our way and saw many interesting things. He allowed me complete liberty. That I will always remember to his credit. Often at nights we nearly froze. But he was a good hand at finding sleeping places, burrowing into the sides of haystacks, opening up old barns, and suchlike. And he always spread part of his coat over me when he lay down to sleep."

· The Fourth Chapter ·

THE CHILDREN'S HOSPITALITY

BUT the day soon came when my new friend played me false. He wanted money. I fancy it was to get coach fare to go to some other part of the country. I don't know. Anyway one afternoon he knocked at a farmhouse door. I thought that as usual he was going to ask for food. Imagine my horror when he said to the woman who answered the door, 'Do you want to buy a dog, ma'am?'

"I just ran. I left him standing at the door there and never looked back. It was such a shock to my faith in human nature that for the present I did nothing but feel blue. Puzzled, I went on down the road, still seeking my fortune, alone. It was only later that I began to feel angry and indignant. The cheek of the man, trying to sell me when he hadn't even bought me! Me, the free companion of the road who had been in partnership with him! Why, I had caught dozens of rabbits and pheasants for that ungrateful tramp. And that was how he repaid me!

"After jogging miserably along for a few miles I came upon some children playing with a ball. They seemed nice youngsters. I was always fond of ball games and I just joined in this one, chased the ball whenever it rolled away and got it for them. I could see they were delighted to have me and for quite a while we had a very good time together.

"Then the children found it was time to go home to supper. I had no idea where my own supper was coming from, so I decided I'd go along with them. Maybe they would let me join them at their meal too, I thought. They appeared more pleased than ever when I started to follow them. But when they met their mother at the gate and told her that I had played with them and followed them home, she promptly chased me off with a broom. Stray dogs, she said, always had diseases. Goodness only knows where she got that from! *Stray* dogs too, if you please. To her every animal who wasn't tagged onto some stupid human must be a stray, something to be pitied, something disgraceful. Well, anyway, to go on—that night it did seem to me as though mankind were divided into two classes: those that enslaved dogs when they wanted to be free; and those that chased them away when they wanted to be friendly.

"One of the children, a little girl, began to cry when her mother drove me off, saying she was sure I was hungry, which I was. She had more sense than her mother, had that child. However I thought I'd use a little strategy. So I just pretended to go off; but I didn't go far. When the lights were lit in the dining room I waited till I saw the mother's shadow on a blind in another part of the house. I knew then that the children would be alone at their supper. I slipped up to the window, hopped onto the sill, and tapped gently on the pane with my paw. At first the children were a bit scared, I imagine. But presently one of them came

"She promptly chased me off with a broom"

over, raised the corner of the blind, and saw me squatting on the sill outside.

"Well, to make a long story short, the youngsters not only took me in but they stowed me away in a closet so their mother wouldn't see me and gave me a fine square meal into the bargain. And after they were supposed to be fast asleep one of them crept downstairs and took me up to their nursery where I slept under a bed on a grand soft pillow that they spread for me. That was what I call hospitality. Never was a tramp dog treated better.

"One of them crept downstairs"

"In the morning I managed to slip out unseen by Mama and once more I hit the trail. Not only was one child crying this time but the whole four of them were sniffling at the garden gate as I said good-bye. I often look back on those children's hospitality as one of the happiest episodes in my entire career. They certainly knew how to treat dogs —and such people, as we all know, are scarce. I hated to leave them. And I don't believe I would have done if it hadn't been for their mama and her insulting remark about all stray dogs having diseases. That was too much.

So, with a good plate of oatmeal porridge and gravy inside me—which the children had secretly given me for breakfast—I faced the future with a stout heart and wondered as I trotted along the highway what Fortune would bring forward next."

· The Fifth Chapter ·

GYPSY LIFE

ABOUT three miles farther on I overtook a Gypsy caravan creeping along the road through the morning mist. At the rear of the procession a dog was scouting around in the ditches for rats. I had never met a Gypsy dog, so, rather curious, I went up to him and offered to help him hunt for rats. He seemed a sort of a grouchy silent fellow, but I liked him, for all that. He made no objection to my joining him and together we gave several rats a good run for their money.

"Little by little I drew the Gypsy dog out and questioned him as to what sort of a life it was to travel with the caravans. These people too were folk of the road like me, and I had serious thoughts of throwing in my lot with them for a while. From what he told me I gathered that a dog led quite a free life with the Gypsies and was interfered with very little.

" 'The group is kind of irregular,' said my friend, who had now gotten over his grouchiness somewhat and seemed inclined to take to me. 'But then the whole of the

Gypsy business is irregular, one might say. If you can stand that you'll probably rather like the life. It's interesting, traveling around all the time. We do see the world, after all. If we have hardships, at least it's better than being treated like a lapdog, trotted out on a leash and living on the same street all the time. Why don't you try it for a while? Just tag along with me. No one will mind. Likely as not, the Gypsies themselves will never even notice that you've joined the caravan—at least not for a few days, anyhow.'

"I did not need very much persuasion and it turned out eventually that I did join the Gypsies and on the whole had quite a good time with them. My friend had certainly been right about the food. To say it was irregular was putting it mildly. There were many days and nights when there simply wasn't any. But the Gypsy dog, through long experience in this kind of life, knew all sorts of dodges for getting provender under difficult conditions. I strongly suspect that my friend was one of the cleverest larder burglars that ever lived. Often I didn't even know where he got the supplies from and no amount of questioning would make him tell. Many a night when we were both starving, around suppertime, with the prospect of going to bed hungry beneath the caravans, Mudge would say to me—that was his name, Mudge—'Oh, golly! I'm not going to bed hungry. Listen, Quetch, I think I know where I may be able to raise some fodder. You wait here for me.'

" 'Shall I come too?' I'd say.

" 'Er—no. Better not, I think,' he'd mutter. 'Hunting is sometimes easier single-handed.'

"Then off he would go. And in half an hour he'd be back

"Another time it would be a roast chicken"

again with the most extraordinary things. One night he would bring a steak-and-kidney pudding, tied up in the muslin it was boiled in—complete, mind you, and steaming hot. Another time it would be a roast chicken, stuffed with sage and onions, with sausages skewered to its sides.

"Of course it didn't take much detective work to tell, on occasions of this kind, that Mudge had just bagged someone else's dinner. I'm afraid I was usually far too hungry to waste time moralizing over where the things came from. Still, I strongly suspect that some good housewives called down many curses on Mudge's head during the course of his career. But the marvelous thing to me was how he did it without ever being caught.

"Yet the life was certainly pleasant for the most part. We visited all the fairs and saw the towns in holiday mood. It was in these days that I met Toby, who was, as you know, then a Punch-and-Judy dog. Yes, I liked the Gypsy life—chiefly because we were nearly always in the country, where a dog's life has most fun in it. Along the lanes there were always rats to dig for; across the meadows there were always hares to chase; and in the roadside woods and copses there were always pheasants and partridges to catch.

"That chapter of my life lasted about three months and it ended, as did the one before it, suddenly. We had been visiting a fair in a town of considerable size. Part of our own show was a fortune-telling booth. Here an old Gypsy woman, the mother of our boss, used to tell people's fortunes with cards. A party of quite well-to-do folk stopped at the booth one day to have their fortunes told. Mudge and I were hanging around outside the tent.

" 'Let's get away from here,' he whispered to me. 'I don't like the looks of this mob. I lost a friend like that once before.'

" 'Like what?' I asked.

" 'Oh, Joe,' said Mudge. Joe was the name of our boss. 'Joe never notices any stray dogs who join the caravan till somebody else notices them. Then he tries to sell them . . . This friend of mine was a whippet. One of the visitors to the booth took a fancy to him, and Joe just sold him then and there. I'd never get sold because I'm not nifty-

"I had been looking at the lines in my paw pads"

looking. But you, you're smart enough to catch anyone's eye—especially the women. Take my advice: Fade away till this mob's gone.'

"Mudge was already moving off, but I called him back. I was interested in this fortune-telling business. I hoped to get my own fortune told by the old woman. She read people's palms. I had been looking at the lines in my paw pads and they seemed to me quite unusual. The future interested me. I was keen to know what sort of a career I had before me. I felt it ought to be a great one.

" 'Just a minute, Mudge,' I said. 'Why get worried? How can Joe sell me when I don't belong to him?'

" 'Don't you worry about that,' said Mudge. 'Joe would sell anything, the Houses of Parliament or the coat off the Prime Minister's back—if he could. A word to the wise: Fade away.'

"Mudge's advice was sound, but for me it came a bit late. I noticed as I turned to follow him that one of the women was already pointing at me and that Joe, to whom she was talking, was very interested in the interest she was showing. For about half an hour after that I saw nothing more of Mudge. I had moved around to another part of the fairgrounds till the visitors should have departed from the fortune-telling booth.

"While I was looking at a strong man lifting weights, the Gypsy dog suddenly came up to me from behind and whispered, 'It's all up, Quetch. You'll have to clear out. That woman liked you so much that she said she'd buy you when Joe offered you to her. He is hunting for you everywhere now.'

" 'But why,' I asked, 'can't I just keep out of the way till the woman has gone?'

" 'It is no use,' said Mudge. 'Joe won't rest till he has sold you, now that he knows you're the kind of dog the ladies take a fancy to. What's more, if he misses this sale he will likely keep you on a chain right along, so as to make sure of you next time someone wants to buy you.'

" 'Good gracious, Mudge!' I cried. 'Would he really do that? But tell me, why do you yourself live with such a man? Come with me and we will go off together.'

"Mudge grinned and shook his head.

" 'Joe is all right to me,' he said. 'He may not be what

"Mudge shook his head"

you'd call exactly a gentleman. But he's all right to me. You're a stranger, you see. He looks on me as one of the tribe, the Romany folk, you understand. Their hand is against every man but not against one another. Even if I were good-looking enough to bring him a ten-pound note I doubt if Joe would sell me. He is a queer one, is Joe. But he's always been square to me . . . No, Quetch, I'll stay with the caravan, with the Romany folk. Once a vagabond, always a vagabond, they say. I'll miss you. But, well . . . Good luck to you, Quetch . . . Better be going now. If Joe once lays hands on you you'll never get away till he sells you—you can be sure of that.'

"So, very sad at heart—for I had grown very fond of the strange Mudge, the Gypsy mongrel, the dog of few words—I left the fair and struck out along the road again, the Road of Fortune, alone.

"Dear me, what an unsatisfactory world it was! When you did find a nice kind of life something or somebody always seemed to shove you out of it just as you were beginning to enjoy it.

"Still, I had much of the world to see yet. And after all, my experiences so far had not brought to me that ideal independent sort of life that I was looking for. I was sorry I had not been able to have my fortune told. I looked at my paw again. I was sure it must be a good one. It was a nice sunny day. I soon threw aside my gloomy thoughts and trotted forward, eager to see what every new turn in the road might bring."

· The Sixth Chapter ·

THE ACROBAT

THAT day I had very bad luck in the matter of food. I hardly got anything to eat all day. By the evening I was positively ravenous. I came to a town. Hoping to pick up bones or scraps that other dogs had left, I searched several backyards. But all I got was two or three fights with wretched, inhospitable curs who objected to my coming into their premises.

"Then, famished and very bored with life, I wandered through the streets. At a corner I came upon an acrobat performing. He was standing on his hands and doing somersaults and things like that. He was all alone. There was a hat laid on the curbstone in front of him, and from time to time people threw coppers into it.

"This set me thinking. The man was evidently making his living this way. In my life with the Gypsies I had often seen dog acts in the circus ring. Some of the tricks I had practiced myself when I had had a notion to go in for a circus career, and I had become skilled in quite a few of them. I could stand on my front paws, beg with a lump of

"I came upon an acrobat performing"

sugar on my nose, throw a back somersault, and so forth. Very well then, I said to myself, why shouldn't I give a one-dog show on the streets of this town, the same as the man was doing? But I needed a hat for the people to throw money into—only in my case I hoped they would throw cutlets and sausages instead. Yes, the first thing to do was to get a hat.

"I knew that hats were to be found in shops and on garbage heaps. I set off and hunted around the backs of houses. The garbage heaps of this town had everything on them *but* hats. Most annoying. Where could I find one? I *must* have a hat. I passed a hat shop. The shopkeeper was busy writing in a book. There were lots of hats on the counter and many more in boxes on the floor. I was desperate. He could easily spare me one—he had so many. I dashed in and tried my luck. Bother it! I couldn't get the hat out of the box quick enough. The shopkeeper threw his book at me and chased me out.

"I went on down the street.

"Never mind, I said to myself. I'll get a hat, somehow, yet.

"As I turned the corner into another street I saw an old gentleman crossing the road. He was all muffled up and full of dignity. And on his head he had an elegant high hat —just the kind of hat I wanted for my performance.

"Ah! I said to myself. If I can only trip that old gentleman up, his hat will roll off, and I can take it to another part of the town and begin my show.

"No sooner said than done. I leapt out into the road and ran between his feet. He stumbled and came down with a grunt on his stomach. His hat rolled into the gutter. I grabbed it and shot off down the street. Before the old gentleman had time to pick himself up I was around the corner and out of sight.

"I didn't stop running till I got to an entirely different part of the town, quite a distance away. Here I felt I was safe from pursuit. I found myself at a busy street corner.

"Now, I thought, the next thing is to collect a crowd.

"I set the top hat on the curbstone, got inside it, and started barking for all I was worth. Very soon passersby began to stop and wonder what it was all about. I went on yelping—I was sorry I hadn't a drum; that's what I should

"I got inside it and started barking"

have had. Then I got out of the high hat, bowed to the audience, and began my show. I begged, stood on my front paws, threw somersaults, etc. It was quite as good a show as the acrobat had given—better, in fact.

"The audience didn't know quite what to make of it. They gaped and gaped. Then they began asking one another, 'Where's his master? . . . who's he with?'

"The silly people couldn't believe I was my own master, giving my own show. After a little they came to the conclusion it was some new trick, that my master had hidden himself somewhere near and was just proving how wonderfully I had been trained by not appearing on the scene himself till after the performance was over. Then pennies began dropping into the hat. That was all very well, but I couldn't eat pennies.

"However the crowd finally did realize that I was entirely on my own. And some old ladies in the audience, instead of giving me coins, took their money into a butcher's shop nearby and bought some meat to give me. This I gobbled up with great relish and they went and got some more. The crowd grew bigger and bigger meanwhile. And pretty soon, eating between somersaults, I was as full as an egg and I couldn't have done another trick if you had given me a kingdom.

"Well, my act earned me a very square meal, but it also nearly cost me my liberty. Why is it that people just can't seem to understand that a dog may be satisfied to be his own boss? Before my show had gone very far many well-meaning people among the audience decided they ought to adopt me.

" '*Such* a clever little dog!' cried one old lady. 'I think I'll take him home with me—that is, if no one really owns him. Did you see the way he ate those sausages I gave him? He must be starving. He ought to have a good home, such a clever dog.'

"At that I made up my mind to close my act in a hurry. But it wasn't at all easy to get away, I found. By this time I had attracted such a crowd at the corner that the traffic was held up. People were jammed in around me like a solid wall. Several persons in the audience began to argue as to which of them should adopt me. I should have been

"Emptying the meat out of it"

flattered, no doubt, but I wasn't. I looked around frantically for a means of escape.

"Then suddenly the old gentleman whose hat I had stolen came up on the outskirts of the throng and recognized his topper, filled with pieces of meat and calves' liver, sitting on the curbstone. Furious with rage he began milling his way in through the mob. While he was picking up his hat and emptying the meat out of it—I hadn't been able to eat more than half of the crowd's contributions—I scuttled out through the lane he had made coming in. The people's attention was suddenly turned to his lamentations and the story of how I had stolen his hat. And while they were listening I got through into more open country in the middle of the street.

"But the crowd was not long in missing me.

" 'Stop him! Grab him! He's getting away!' someone called.

"And then as I bolted round the corner I realized that I had the whole town chasing me.

"I had eaten so many sausages and veal kidneys and pork chops that running at all was no easy matter. However, I saw plainly that if I was going to keep my treasured liberty I had got to put my best foot forward.

"Luckily it was quite dark now. And as soon as I got off the main thoroughfares, away from the shops and into the dimly lit back streets, I soon gave the crowd the slip.

"Ten minutes later, when I slowed down on the open road again outside the town, I said to myself, Well, I earned my own living tonight, all right. But next time I do it I'll try some other way."

· The Seventh Chapter ·

THE MONASTERY

QUETCH'S story had now been going on for some hours. And the attention of the audience had not slackened in the least. For my part, while my fingers felt a bit stiff from writer's cramp (for you must remember I was taking down all these stories in shorthand, to be put into the book, *Tales of the Home for Crossbred Dogs*), I was still too deeply absorbed in the history of this strange little terrier to bother about the time. Neither had it occurred to the Doctor to look at his watch. And it is quite likely that we would all have sat on there listening till the cocks crowed if Dab-Dab had not suddenly appeared and told us that it was long after midnight and high time that the Doctor was abed.

So the rest of "The Story of the Dog Who Set Out to Seek His Fortune" was put off till the following night.

But when the next evening came I could see by the eager way the crowd got ready to listen that the delay had only made them that much keener to hear the remainder of it.

"The next chapter in my story," Quetch continued, "was

"Dab-Dab suddenly appeared"

rather odd—peaceful but odd. The colder weather was coming on—for it was late in the year. When I felt that I was well beyond the reach of pursuit of the angry old gentleman and the townsfolk, I began to keep an eye open for a decent place to sleep. The best I could find was a haystack, into which I burrowed a sort of hole and curled myself up inside. I was just about to drop off when a biting, cold wind sprang up in the east and began blowing right into my little den. I soon realized that I had got to make a move. I tried the other side of the stack, but it wasn't much better. So I decided to go on down the road and find another place.

"I hadn't gone very far when I heard a bell tolling. I peered into the darkness off to the side of the road and saw a large stone building. At one end there was a sort of chapel with stained glass windows, dimly lighted. It was the only habitation in the neighborhood, standing in the midst of its own grounds, apparently. I went up closer and saw that there were men dressed in robes solemnly gathering in the little chapel. It was evidently a monastery. I knew, because there had been one near our home farm. These monks would be going into vespers, the evening service.

"Well, I was never what you would call a religious dog. On the other hand, no one could call me bigoted or intolerant. Among my friends upon the Scotch farm I had had Episcopalian, Presbyterian, Methodist, and Baptist dogs. One of my closest chums had been an Airedale who belonged to a Jewish rabbi. The little chapel looked warm and inviting compared to the cold night outside. The doors would soon close. I joined the procession and went in to vespers.

"Well, it seemed that some of the monks were not as broad-minded about matters of religion as I myself. They objected to my coming in. I suppose they thought I wasn't a Roman Catholic dog and hadn't any business there. Anyway, I had no sooner found an empty pew, free from drafts, and curled myself up to listen to the service in comfort, than I was grabbed by one of the lay brothers, carried to the door, and put out.

"I was greatly shocked by this. I had always understood that monasteries were famous for their hospitality. What sort was this, when a gentleman of the road, taking shelter from a windy night within their walls, was grabbed by the scruff of the neck and shoved out into the cold? While I was wondering what I would do next, the organ started playing and the monks began singing psalms. Such voices, my gracious! I could do better myself. I would show them. I leaned against the chapel door and joined in the chorus. Of course I couldn't sing the words. But I had no difficulty in following the general lines of the tune quite as musically as they were doing.

"To my surprise, my joining the choir seemed to stop the organ. Next I heard whisperings behind the closed door of the chapel.

" 'Perhaps it is the devil, Brother Francis,' I heard one monk say, 'trying to disturb us at our devotions. Do not open the door on any account.'

"This wasn't very flattering, nor in the least helpful. But presently the abbot—that is, the head of the monks—came down to the door of the chapel to see what all the disturbance was about. The abbot was a very fine man. He became, afterwards, a great friend of mine. Devil or no devil, the abbot believed in facing the problems of life. He ordered the door to be opened at once. He smiled when he saw me sitting on the step outside.

" 'Come in, stranger,' said he, 'and take shelter from the wind and cold.'

"I didn't wait for any second invitation but trotted in at once and made myself comfortable in one of the pews. Several of the monks looked kind of shocked and scandalized. But as it was their own abbot who had let me in, there wasn't anything they could do about it. Then they went on with the service.

"I joined in the chorus"

"After it was over they all started to troop out again. They were very solemn and serious. I joined the procession, sticking close to the abbot, who was, I realized, a good person to keep in with. From the door of the chapel, two by two, with our eyes on the ground, we traipsed along a stone-paved cloister and entered another door. Beyond this, I was delighted to discover, lay the dining room, or refectory, as it is always called in monasteries. Good cooking smells greeted our nostrils. With the cold, nippy wind I already had a great appetite again.

"Many was the jolly run we had together"

"Well, I followed the monastic life for several months. It wasn't half bad. The monks were a very nice lot of men when you got to know them. And as soon as I was accepted into the order I was allowed to go everywhere and do pretty much as I pleased. In that respect it was one of the freest, most agreeable chapters in my whole career. The old abbot was lots of fun. Naturally of a very cheerful disposition, he often had, I could see, very hard work keeping up the solemn dignity that seemed to be expected of his position as head of the monastery. I am sure that he found in his friendship for me a chance to let off steam and be natural. Many was the jolly run we had together, down in a hollow of the monastery meadows where no one could see us, in pursuit of an otter or a hare.

"Of course it *was* quiet—there's no denying that. Prayers, digging in the garden, farm and house work were all we did; and day followed day in peaceful sameness. But for my part I managed to get a good deal of fun out of it. In return for my board and lodging I kept the monastery and the farm buildings free from rats. That gave me plenty to do. And it was about this time that I first became a collector. The abbot was a geologist and he used to collect stones and pieces of rock. I helped him in digging for them.

"Yes, I had a very peaceful life while I was a monk dog. I would probably have stayed with it much longer if it had not been for my desire to see more of the world. This finally led me to bid farewell to the monastery and its nice abbot and set forth once more upon my wanderings."

· The Eighth Chapter ·
THE SHEPHERD IN DISTRESS

THE winter was now in full swing and it was not a good season to be homeless. For a week or two I spent about the hardest time that I have ever gone through. Icy blizzards were blowing most of the time. When I wasn't nearly frozen I was almost starved to death.

"One day when I was down to a very low level of misery and want, trudging along the road wondering where my next meal was coming from, I saw a shepherd having a hard time rounding up his flock. He had a sheepdog with him, but the animal was a fool and no good at the business.

"I was awfully weak for want of food, but I saw here a chance of something worthwhile. The shepherd was in despair. The wind was blowing like a crazy hurricane, now this way, now that. Darkness was coming on. The sheep were scattered in all directions, scared by the gale. The man's dog was more a nuisance than a help. He tried hard enough, but he just didn't know the business of sheepherding. Having helped my father on the home farm—he was one of the best sheepdogs that ever barked, even if he was only a terrier—I did know something about it.

"After a little the poor shepherd saw that his dog was worse than useless and he whistled and called him off the job. That was my chance. In less time than it takes to tell, I shot around that flock and herded it up through the gate that I saw the shepherd was trying to pass it through. Once I had the sheep in the fenced enclosure the job was done and the shepherd was happy. I came up to him wagging my tail. He fell on my neck and almost wept. If that flock had been lost in the night storm I suppose he would have got into serious trouble.

"That was how I started two friendships that lasted a long while—one with the shepherd, the other with his dog. I went home with the two of them that night and was rewarded with a good hearty meal of stew and a warm bed. While supper was being prepared I heard the shepherd telling his wife how, when it looked as though the flock would be surely lost, I had appeared on the scene and saved the day.

"But the curious thing about this incident was that the shepherd, by no means an educated person, never tried to take advantage of me, restrict my liberty, or capture me as his property. I suppose, being a sheepherder himself, he recognized in me an expert in his own trade who was entitled to respect. In other words, I had, for perhaps the first time in dog history, hired myself out as an independent specialist and could leave or stay with the job as I pleased.

"Poor though he was, the man gave me splendid meals, in every way as good as his own. I took his dog in hand—he was a collie, a decent fellow even if he was a bit stupid

"Telling his wife that I had saved the day"

—and taught him over several weeks how sheepherding should be done under varying conditions of weather.

"You know, that game is not quite as easy as it looks to the man who passes by. Sheep are a herd animal—very much a herd animal. If the weather is fine they behave one way; if it is rough they behave another; if it is hot they do this; if it rains they do that—and so forth. Now if you're a sheepdog—a good sheepdog—you've got to know these things and act accordingly.

"Well, anyway, I put the shepherd's dog through a

regular course. I enjoyed it myself—as one always does when teaching the other fellow. By the end of a fortnight poor Raggles, as he was called, was a really good sheepdog and could be trusted to take care of a flock even if a blizzard sprang up at twilight, which is perhaps the hardest thing that a sheepdog is ever called upon to do."

· The Ninth Chapter ·

CITY LIFE

BUT my yearning to see the world led me to drop that too, just as it had the peace of the monastic life. And the day came when I said good-bye to the shepherd and his dog and set out once more. It had been kind of lonely on the sheep farm and I thought I would like to try city life for a while. I journeyed on till I came to a big town. You see, being still pretty inexperienced, I thought it would be quite a simple matter for a dog to go to a city and take up his residence there like a person. But I discovered it wasn't.

"Firstly, finding a place to live was hard. I solved that problem eventually by taking up my quarters in an old packing case that I found in an empty lot. It was one of those places where people dump rubbish. The packing case, as a kennel, left a good deal to be desired, but it might have been worse. The wind and the rain blew in through the holes of it. But it was much better after I had stuffed it and lined it with some straw and rags, which I found nearby among the rubbish.

"Another problem was the food. This was always sort of

"The packing case as a kennel left a good deal to be desired"

hard. But I had supposed it would be easier in a city where so many had to be fed and such a lot of food was on sale. But, on the contrary, I never met with such extraordinary difficulty in getting enough to eat.

"However the worst thing of all was the dogcatchers. In cities, I discovered, homeless dogs are not allowed. By homeless they mean ownerless. An office called the Department of Public Health is responsible for this. It is not supposed to be healthy for a town to have ownerless dogs knocking around its streets.

"Of all the inhospitable, unfriendly institutions, that of town dogcatchers is I think the worst. The idea is this: A man with a wagon goes around the streets. And any dogs he finds who haven't collars on or who appear to be without masters or lost get grabbed by the dogcatcher and put into his wagon. Then they are taken to a place and kept there to see if anyone wishes to claim them or adopt them. After a certain number of days, if no one has come forward to give them a home, they are destroyed.

"Dear me, what a time I had keeping out of the clutches of those dogcatchers! I seemed to be always getting chased. Life just wasn't worth living. Although I managed to get away I finally decided that a town was no place for me and that I didn't care for city life at all.

"And then just as I was preparing to leave one evening I *did* get caught. Goodness, how scared I was! As the wretched old wagon rumbled along over the cobbled streets I cowered inside, thinking that the end of my career had surely come. At the home, or whatever it was called where we were taken, we were treated quite kindly, as a matter of fact—fed well and given decent beds. Well, there I waited in the greatest anxiety, wondering whether I was going to get adopted or not.

"On the third day, which I believe was the last day of grace allowed, an old lady called at the home. It seemed it was a habit of hers, calling to see if she could rescue any stray dogs from destruction. Her keen old eyes picked me out right away.

" 'Oh,' said she, 'he looks like a nice dog, that Aberdeen over there. I think I can find a home for him.'

"Then she asked the man in charge to keep me till the

"An old lady called"

next day, when she hoped to be able to bring someone along who would adopt me.

"This she did. He was a funny sort of man, harmless enough. He took me away with a piece of string tied around my neck. And I assure you I was glad enough to go with him.

"After I got to his home I decided that he wasn't very anxious to have me, really, after all. I felt that most likely he had only taken me to oblige the old lady. He was one of those fussy bachelors, worse than any old maid—had to have everything in his house in apple-pie order and nearly had a fit if I got onto the chairs or left hairs on the hearth-rug.

"After staying with him a week I made up my mind that he would probably be greatly relieved if I ran away and freed him of my company. Which I did, choosing the nighttime for my departure so that I could get out of the town without running into those wretched dogcatchers again."

· The Tenth Chapter ·

THE HERMIT DOG

THIS time I determined to remove myself from the haunts of Man completely and entirely.

"To find a piece of country that was wild enough for my purpose was not easy. I made inquiries of dogs whom I met along the roads. They told me of certain big forests and heaths where they reckoned that a dog could live, hidden away in peace, if he wanted to. These districts were all quite a distance off. I chose one that sounded the best and started out to get there.

"It took me three days of steady travel. On the way the countryside grew less and less peopled; and when at last I came to the part I was making for, it certainly was lonesome and desolate enough for anything. Some of it was mountainous. For the rest, wide expanses of forest and brambly rolling heath sheltered only the timid native creatures of the wild. One couldn't find a better place for a dog to lead a hermit's life.

"I began by making a thorough exploration of the whole section till I knew every dell and thicket in it. Then I found a fine old hollow tree, like a bear's den, which made the snuggest home you ever saw. No winds or storms could reach me there, and it was as dry as any house or kennel. It was situated in one of the remotest and thickest parts of the forest where no stray traveler would be likely to find me—even supposing that any stray travelers ever passed that way. Quite near there was a splendid little mountain brook where I could always get a drink. Rabbits seemed plentiful, partridges, and woodcock too; and there were a few squirrels and small game. Even in the winter season the woods were full of wonderful smells and looked very attractive.

"So, I said to myself the first evening when I brought home a rabbit to my lair and prepared to turn in for the night—so! What do I care now for Man and his silly civilization? Here I will settle down, a wild dog, independent and self-reliant, living on the wilderness as did my forefathers before me. This is the life! Let Man go hang!

"Well, I stuck to my experiment long enough to prove it could be done. Entirely self-supporting and independent, I lived in the woods through the rest of the winter. Hardships I had in plenty; but I did it. Of course my diet was almost always raw meat, occasionally fish when I managed to catch the big trout drowsing in the rocky pools of the mountain brook. But that wasn't often. They were clever customers and were seldom off their guard. But I did get one or two a week—after I had secretly watched how the otters managed it, lying on the banks among the bracken, motionless for hours, and then, when the chance came, plunging right into the icy waters like a fish myself and battling with them in their own element. I learned a

"I found a fine old hollow tree"

lot of hunting dodges from the otters—and from the weasels, too.

"In many ways it was indeed a great life. But suddenly after a while I found I wasn't really contented. I found myself wandering off to the few lonely little farms whose pastures bordered the heathlands beyond the edge of the forest. I didn't know why I did this at first. But soon I realized that I wanted to see and talk with other dogs. One farm dog I persuaded to leave his home and come and live with me. Together we had a very good time and he enjoyed

"Battling with them in their own element"

it no end when I showed him how the independent wild life could be lived and taught him a lot of the hunting lore I had learned from the otters and foxes. And then too, hunting with a partner was of course much easier than hunting alone.

"But after a few weeks we both got sort of mopy. It perplexed us a good deal till finally we talked it over together and came to the conclusion that perhaps we wanted to be among people again. We both started remembering what good times we had had with this farmer or that shepherd or those children, going for walks, playing games, ratting together, and so forth.

"One evening my friend said to me, 'You know, Quetch, the trouble is we *can* live alone, the same as the wild animals. But I don't believe we want to—not for long, anyway. Our ancestors have lived for so many generations as part of the human household that now we miss the things that mankind's company has provided us with. There was a small boy back on that farm I left—as funny a little tow-haired scrub as ever you laid eyes on. I never thought I'd miss him, never. He used to take me with him when he went to look for mushrooms in the fall or for birds' nests or water lilies in the spring. And now—it's funny—I find myself longing to see him again . . . Would you mind very much, Quetch, if I left you and went back?'

"Well, what could I answer? When he asked me that question I realized at once that the end of the experiment had come for me as well as for him. Life in the wild alone, after I had shared it with him, would have been quite unbearable for me.

" 'All right,' I said. 'Maybe I'm more independently inclined than most dogs. But there is a great deal in what you say. Nevertheless, if I go back to Man and his civilization I will only do it on certain conditions. I must be allowed to be my own boss. I will *not* be chained up and made to keep a whole lot of rules.'

" 'In that case, why don't you go and try to get into the Doctor's club?' said he.

" 'Doctor? Club?' I asked. 'I don't follow you. What doctor? What club?'

" 'Well,' said my friend, 'I don't know just where he lives, but almost any dog you meet seems to have heard of him.

" 'Why don't you try to get into the Doctor's club?' "

Dolittle is his name—lives somewhere down in the West Country, as far as I can make out. Must be a very remarkable person, from all reports. Has a club for dogs that is run by the dogs themselves. Certain rules, of course, but only those that the members realize are necessary and lay down. Why don't you try and find him?'

"So that was how I first heard of Doctor Dolittle and his Home for Crossbred Dogs. Right away I realized it was the kind of place I had been looking for all my life up to this—where dogs were allowed to be themselves, and yet where they could enjoy human company on a proper footing, as well.

"When my friend set out I went with him. I had no regrets over leaving my woodland home, in spite of its being such a wonderful spot. At his farm we parted and I went on. As yet of course the neighborhood was very wild and lonely, and there were not many dogs to ask directions from. But soon I came to villages and towns. All the dogs I questioned seemed to have heard of John Dolittle all right, but none of them could give me very definite instructions as to how to reach his home. Some said he might be abroad because he traveled a great deal. I avoided the larger towns as I was still afraid of the dogcatchers. Most of the information given me spoke of the Doctor as living in the West Country; and I kept traveling in that direction all the time.

"In my wanderings I eventually came to a town that was neither very large nor very small. In the market square I saw a Punch-and-Judy show going on. This form of entertainment had always amused me and I stopped to watch it. Presently another dog came up to me from behind and called me by name. Turning, I was delighted to find my old friend Toby. He had been watching the performance with a professional interest.

"We got chatting and I asked him if he had ever heard of this John Dolittle. You can imagine how glad I was to learn that not only was Toby living with the great man himself but that this town that I had come to was none other than Puddleby-on-the-Marsh, where the Doctor had his home. Toby volunteered to take me around there to see if he could get me into the celebrated club.

"And so there came an end to my wanderings. I had been

"I saw a Punch-and-Judy show going on"

a tramp dog, a performing dog, a Gypsy dog, a monk dog, a professional sheepherder, and a hermit wild dog. Not a very exciting career, perhaps, but at least it had plenty of variety in it. I can assure you I was very glad to settle down in these pleasant surroundings"—Quetch waved an expressive paw toward the wide dining room and the gymnasium that lay beyond the double doors—"which are certainly my idea of a comfortable independent life. I hope the club continues to flourish for many years and I thank you for the attention with which you have listened to my story."

· The Eleventh Chapter ·

THE TOPKNOT TERRIERS

PROFESSOR QUETCH was given quite as much applause as any storyteller who had gone before him. When it had subsided Jip, as president of the club, got up to thank him formally on behalf of the audience.

This over, Jip went on to say that since no story had yet been slated to follow Quetch's, he would like to know if any members had suggestions to make about filling out the remainder of the evening's entertainment.

Then one dog got up (he was a cross between a St. Bernard and a mastiff) and said that he thought a story about the Doctor would be a good idea.

Jip agreed that this was a good idea. Then he started to count off the dogs, besides himself, who had lived a considerable time with the Doctor. There was Swizzle the clown dog, Toby the Punch-and-Judy dog, Kling the detective dog, Blackie the retriever, and Grab the bulldog. Each of these in turn was asked if he could think of any incident in his life with the Doctor that would make a good story.

Then the sea dog got up and said, "I think that Jip himself, who has, after all, known John Dolittle longer than any of us, ought to tell us a story about the Doctor."

"All right," said Jip. "In that case I think I'll tell you the story of how John Dolittle invented the topknot terrier. You know then, of course, that the Doctor has never cared very much whether a dog was what is known as a thoroughbred. Whether a dog had a nice personality or was intelligent was far more important to him. Well, some years ago there was a certain rich and highborn lady known as the Dowager Countess of Battlebridge, who realized that the Doctor was a great man. This was curious because people, as a class, usually think him something of a crank. That, as many of you know, has always had the effect of making him keep very much to himself and the animal world. But the Dowager Countess of Battlebridge was an exception—an exceptional woman all around, in fact. She was extremely interested in, and fond of, animals and she had a great admiration for the Doctor's knowledge of animal medicine. She did not, any more than the rest of the world, believe that he could talk animal languages. But she saw that he certainly had a great gift for communicating ideas to them and getting them to understand what he wanted. She had a whole lot of dogs of her own and was a great authority on breeds, attending all the shows, where she was very often one of the judges.

"Whenever any of her animals were sick she always got the Doctor to attend to them, maintaining that he was the only veterinary surgeon in the country worthy of the title. Among her dogs she had one very jolly little poodle called Juanita—frightfully thoroughbred, prizewinner, and all that.

"One day Juanita was missing. The dowager countess

"The dowager countess was in despair"

was in despair. She put advertisements in all the papers, hired detectives to hunt for the dog, and everything. All to no purpose. Juanita the prize poodle had disappeared as completely as though the earth had opened and swallowed her up.

"One evening when I and the Doctor were in the study we heard a tapping at the window. I knew that tap. I had heard it before. It was Cheapside the cockney sparrow knocking on the glass with his bill.

" 'Well, Doctor,' says he as soon as he was let in, 'where

"It was Cheapside knocking on the glass with his bill"

do you think Juanita the prize poodle is hiding? In your stable.'

"'In my stable!' cried the Doctor. 'What a place to choose, when she had the most luxurious home in the country to live in!'

"'Yes, but listen, Doctor,' says Cheapside, coming closer and lowering his voice. 'That isn't all. She's got puppies—five of 'em, the queerest little things you ever saw. They've got topknots on their heads. Look like a cross between a weasel and a pincushion. I reckon she's ashamed of 'em, is

Juanita—being they're so queer-looking—and that's why she has kept in hiding.'

" 'Oh, well,' said the Doctor, 'let's go down and take a look at them right away.'

"Thereupon we all proceeded to the stable with a lantern. And under an old manger, among some straw and autumn leaves, we found Juanita and her family. I am bound to say that Cheapside's description had not been in the least exaggerated. They *were* queer. At first I could scarcely believe they were dogs at all. It was only by the smell of them that I was sure.

" 'My goodness, Juanita,' said the Doctor, 'why didn't you let me know you were here all the time?'

" 'Well,' said she, 'for one thing I didn't want to put you in an embarrassing position with regard to the countess. And for another, I—er—I—er—'

"She looked at the queer puppies and paused. She seemed dreadfully awkward and ill at ease.

" 'They're hardly thoroughbred, you see, Doctor,' she said at last. 'I didn't know what my mistress would say or do about them. Frankly, I was scared. The countess, as you know, only has dogs of the highest pedigree in her kennels.'

" 'Well,' said the Doctor, '*I* think they are a very jolly-looking lot. These topknots are unique—and very smart, in my opinion. Are they intelligent?'

" 'Oh, yes, indeed,' said Juanita, brightening up and showing no end of motherly pride. 'They're the cleverest lot of puppies I ever had.'

"That, as you can imagine, got the Doctor more interested than anything she could have said. And finally he became tremendously keen on these queer puppies—so keen that he took them across from the stable to his house, where they made themselves a great nuisance to Dab-Dab the housekeeper. They ran all over the place and you stumbled on them everywhere you went.

"Nevertheless there was no denying that they were, as the Doctor had said, distinctly unusual. Clever wasn't the word for them: they were positively uncanny. I have never seen anything like it. Usually it takes a dog years to learn anything about human speech and what it means—if indeed he ever does. But these little beggars seemed to catch on to all that was happening or being said in any language right away.

"Dab-Dab continued to storm and insisted that they be put back in the stable, but the Doctor said, 'No, Dab-Dab. These pups are an extraordinary case of animal intelligence. They must stay. I want to study them. Why, they have real brains, Dab-Dab—*real brains!*'

" 'They're mongrels,' she snapped, 'homely mongrels, at that.'

" 'I don't care,' said the Doctor. 'They represent a distinct advance in animal intelligence.'

"Juanita, who had up to this been scared and ashamed about how they would be received, now began to put on no end of airs as the mother of the most intelligent puppies on record. The Doctor gave them all sorts of tests to demonstrate how clever they were. I do believe that he had hopes of some day getting them to take up mathematics and science—if not to run for Parliament. He was quite excited and worked up over it.

"Not a great while after Juanita's presence in the stable had been announced by Cheapside, the Doctor felt that he

" 'Why, they have real brains, Dab-Dab!' "

ought to notify the Dowager Countess of Battlebridge, for she was still very disturbed over her prize poodle's disappearance. The good lady was overjoyed at the news and immediately asked that Juanita be restored to her home. But the poor puppies, since they were not thoroughbred, she was not in the least interested in. Then the Doctor took two whole hours trying to explain to her that she was wrong.

" 'Don't you see,' said he, 'how much more important it is that Juanita has brought an unusually intelligent kind of a dog into the world than that her children should carry on some set type of breed?'

"Well, the Doctor, after talking very enthusiastically for quite a while about the brilliant intellects of these puppies, got the countess herself interested too. She asked to see them. And the Doctor took her over to the house at once to show them to her.

"And it didn't take those pups long to win the countess's heart. But after she had raved over them a while she seemed a bit ashamed of herself.

" 'Oh, but just *look* at them, Doctor!' she cried, 'with these delightfully absurd, woolly mops on their heads. They're darlings, but they're mongrels. I'd be ashamed to have them in the house.'

" 'Yes, I know. But, after all,' said the Doctor, "breed in dogs is a very artificial thing. Hardly any of the breeds that are popular today are pure native dogs. The bullterrier, the Pomeranian, the black-and-tan: they have all been produced by cross-breeding in the first instance. The only true original breeds are the Eskimo sled dog, the dingo of Australia, and one or two more. Now what I was going to suggest is this: You are a famous authority on dogs with society and the Kennel Club. It is within your power to popularize this new breed that Juanita has given to the world and make it the vogue of the day. Why, only last month Sir Barnaby Scrogley produced a new breed that he called the bobtailed Bolivian beagle. It has since become quite fashionable. His breed hasn't the wits of a cockroach —I know because I've talked with them. Whereas these puppies of Juanita's surpass anything in dog intelligence I ever met.'

"This set the countess thinking. As a matter of fact she

was quite jealous of Lady Scrogley, Sir Barnaby's wife, who was another well-known woman authority on dogs and frequently acted as judge at the Kennel Club shows. The idea of producing a new breed that should outshine, as the fad of the moment, the Scrogleys' Bolivian beagles appealed to the dowager countess immensely.

" 'Humph!' she said at last. 'And what, Doctor, would you call this breed? It doesn't look like anything that has ever been registered so far on the Kennel Club's books.'

" 'We'd call it the topknot terrier,' said John Dolittle. 'A smart name for a very smart dog. I'm sure they would be popular.'

" 'Humph!' said the countess again. 'Perhaps you're right. They certainly are awfully attractive mites . . . Well—er—you must give me a little time to think it over.'

"The next day the countess called on the Doctor and told him that she had decided to follow his suggestion. The puppies were all brushed and combed and their topknots were trimmed (by a French barber) into a very smart shape. They were then taken over to the countess's mansion and adopted into the household with all due ceremony and honor.

"The result of this was exactly as the Doctor had predicted. They became the rage in a week. The dowager countess took one or two with her everywhere she went. And since she was such a very important figure in sporting society these unusual dogs were remarked upon, talked about, and written up in the papers. Everyone wanted to know what the breed was and was told: the topknot terrier. It was repeated everywhere. But the countess went the Doctor one better. Seeing that the Scrogleys had produced a breed of beagles from Bolivia, she wove a wonderful

" 'We'd call it the topknot terrier' "

story about the topknots coming from some remote island in the South Seas. And they finally became known as the 'Fijian topknots.' And if you claimed to be in fashion, *not* to have a Fijian topknot just put you outside the pale instantly. The countess was besieged with letters inquiring about the breed—where could they be obtained, what were they fed on, etc., etc.

"She was delighted—because not only did her new breed entirely outshine the Scrogleys' Bolivian beagles but it earned its popularity by real brains and natural charm.

"Their topknots were trimmed into a very smart shape"

The Fijian topknots were known to be able to do anything short of bookkeeping and astronomy. Also, for the present anyhow, they were nearly priceless—because there were only five of them and all the fashionable ladies in the land were falling over one another to buy them.

"The Doctor was very pleased, for, in its way, this was a great triumph.

" 'That just shows you, Jip,' said he to me one evening, as he was reading his newspaper in front of the fire, 'how utterly absurd is this idea of thoroughbredness in dogs being so much more desirable than cross-breeding. Here we have made a regular mongrel into the last word of up-to-dateness. And all because we called in the aid of a few *society* people. The whole thing is just a question of fashion, Jip. Just fashion—nothing more.' "

PART TWO

· The First Chapter ·

INSECT LANGUAGES

FOR years and years the Doctor had been patiently working on the study of insect languages. He had butterfly-breeding houses where the caterpillars of moths and butterflies were hatched out and liberated in a special enclosed garden, about the size of a room, full of flowers and everything needed for butterfly happiness.

Then hornets, wasps, bees, and ants—we had other special apparatus and homes for them, too. Everything was designed with one foremost idea in view: to keep the insects happy and in normal conditions while they were being studied.

And the water-born creatures, like the dragonflies, the stone flies, etc. —for them he had hundreds of small aquarium tanks with plants and grasses growing in them. Beetles, the same way. In fact there was practically no branch or department of insect life that the Doctor had not at one time or another studied with a view to establishing language contact with it. He had built many delicate machines that he called listening apparatuses.

But in spite of a tremendous amount of patient labor,

"The moths and butterflies were liberated in an enclosed garden"

trial, and experiment, he had admitted to me that he felt he had accomplished nothing. So you can imagine my surprise when he came rushing into the dogs' dining room, grabbed me by the arm, and breathlessly asked me to come with him. Together we ran across to the insect houses. There, over the various listening apparatuses, he attempted to explain to me how he had at last achieved results—results that, he was confidently sure, would lead to his dream being realized.

It was all highly scientific and complicated, and I am afraid that I did not understand a great deal of it. It seemed mostly about "vibrations per second," "sound waves," and the like. As usual with him on such occasions, everything else was laid aside and forgotten in his enthusiasm.

"Stubbins," said he, "I shall need your help for the secretarial work and the note-keeping—there's a tremendous lot of recording to be done. I am overwhelmed by my results. It all came at once—so suddenly. In one swoop I established what I believe are the beginnings of language contact with five different kinds of insects: a wasp, a caterpillar—or, rather, a maggot—a housefly, a moth, and a water beetle. If I am right in my surmises, this is the greatest moment in my whole career. Let us go to work."

And then for many days—and most of the nights, too—we labored. Goodness, how we worked!

The Doctor brought insects into the house in pails, in biscuit tins, in teacups, in everything. You never saw such a mess. His bedroom, the kitchen, the parlor, the study—everywhere you went you found pots of maggots, glasses full of wasps, bowls full of water beetles. Not content with that, he kept going out and getting more. We would walk miles and miles across country, armed with collecting boxes, in search of some especially large beetle or some new kind of wasp that he felt sure would be better for experimenting purposes than any he had used so far.

Poor Gub-Gub was continually getting stung by the wasps—indeed, the house seemed full of them. As for Dab-Dab, her indignation every time a new lot of maggots was brought in was quite indescribable. She threw several lots out of the window when the Doctor wasn't looking; but she

"Gub-Gub was continually getting stung by the wasps"

was always brought to account for it. Because John Dolittle, no matter how many messy little cans he had placed around the house, knew immediately if a single one was missing.

· The Second Chapter ·

FOREIGN INSECTS

FOR my part, I cannot truthfully say that I ever got into real, personal, conversational contact with the insect world. But that John Dolittle did there can be no doubt whatever. This I have proof of from things that happened. You cannot make a wasp stand up on its front legs and wave its other four feet in the air unless you know enough wasp language to make him do so. And that—and a great deal more—I have seen the Doctor accomplish.

Of course it was never quite the free and easy exchange of ideas that his talking with the larger animals had come to be. But then insects' ideas are different; and consequently their languages for conveying those ideas are different. With all but the very largest insects, the "listening," as it was called, was done with these quite complicated and very delicate instruments.

All drafts and vibrations had to be carefully shut off. Later on Bumpo and I made a second building especially for this, with a floor so solid that no footfall or shock, no matter how heavy, could jar the apparatuses. It was also

"He asked several birds to make special trips abroad for him"

equipped with a very fine system for heating the atmosphere to exactly the right temperature. For the Doctor had found that most insects are inclined to go to sleep when the temperature falls below what is for them the normal climate of their active season. As a general rule, the hotter it was the more lively they were and the more they talked. But of course the air could not be allowed to get much warmer than full summer heat.

We called it *listening* for convenience. As a matter of fact, it more often consisted of recording vibrations, the pitch of a buzz, the velocity of the wing stroke, and other slight noises and motions which insects make. With some of the very largest ones it was possible to hear the sounds given out with the naked ear. The clearest results that John Dolittle obtained were with imported insects, such as locusts and cicadas of different kinds. How he procured these foreign specimens was rather interesting. He asked several birds to make special trips abroad for him and to bring back the grubs and eggs of grasshoppers, crickets, etc. Then in his incubating boxes at home he hatched out the eggs and grubs into the full-grown insects.

Most of the information that the Doctor gathered from this new study of insect languages was concerned with the natural history of the various species and genera. With this I filled over sixty thick notebooks for him. But we also learned that several kinds of butterflies had considerable imagination. Some of the yarns I suspect were made up for our amusement. Others sounded as though they had the ring of truth to them. However, I will shortly narrate one or two, and then you can judge for yourselves.

· The Third Chapter ·

TANGERINE

ONE of our most interesting insects was a wasp. The Doctor had of course experimented with a considerable number of wasps. But with this one he had achieved better results than with any. The tiny creature seemed highly intelligent, was much given to talking, so long as the room was kept warm; and, after he had gotten used to John Dolittle, would follow him around the house like a pet cat wherever he went. He allowed the Doctor to handle him without apparently ever dreaming of stinging him and seemed happiest when he was allowed to sit on the Doctor's collar about an inch from his right ear. Gub-Gub it was who christened him with a name of his own—*Tangerine.* This was because when the Doctor had been making inquiries of the wasp as to what foods he liked best he had said a certain yellow jam was his favorite. We tried apricot, peach, quince, Victoria plum. But we finally discovered that what he had meant was a marmalade made from tangerine oranges.

He was then presented with his own private jar of mar-

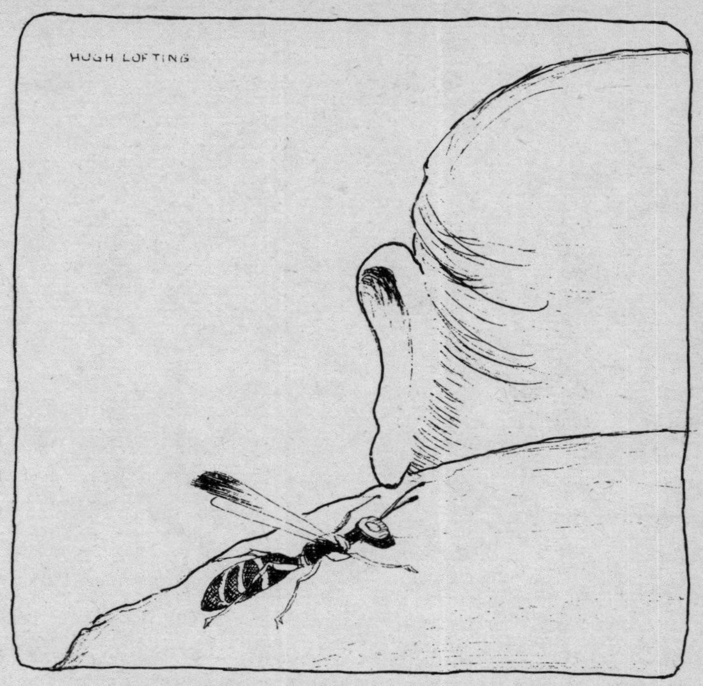

"He seemed happiest when allowed to sit on the Doctor's collar"

malade—with which he seemed greatly delighted. But we saw almost right away that we would have to limit his allowance. He would eat such enormous quantities at one sitting. Then he'd fall asleep and wake up in the morning complaining of a dreadful headache. One evening he ate so much that he fell right into the pot and lay there on his back fast asleep, blissfully drowning in his favorite marmalade. We had to fish him out and give him a warm bath because, of course, his wings and everything were all stuck

"No one else's hands were small enough
to wash a wasp's legs"

together with the jam. In this the white mouse assisted us, as no one else's hands were small enough to wash a wasp's legs and face without doing damage.

This passion for marmalade was Tangerine's only vice—otherwise he seemed to have a very nice disposition, not one that could be called waspish in the least. Gub-Gub, having been stung by wasps before, was dreadfully scared of him. But for the rest of us he had no terrors, beyond a constant anxiety that we might sit on him—since he crawled over all the chairs and sofas and beds in the house as though he owned them.

Among the anecdotes and stories of the insect world that Tangerine related to us, "How I Won the Battle of Bunkerloo" was one of the favorites. And this is how he told it:

"The battlefield of Bunkerloo was situated in a pleasant valley between rolling hills covered with vineyards and olive groves. In the fields and the boles of the olive trees round about there were several wasps' nests. They had always been there—though of course not the same wasps. Yet the traditions and folklore had been handed down from one generation to another. And the thing that we feared and hated most was battles.

"Yes, indeed, war to us was like a red rag to a bull. It seemed such a stupid waste. From either end of our beautiful valley armies would come with cannons and horses and everything. For hours they would shoot off evil-smelling gunpowder, blowing some of the trees right out of the ground by the roots, and destroying simply no end of wasps' nests—some of them quite new ones that we had spent days and weeks in building. Then, after they had fought for hours, they would go away again, leaving hundreds of dead men and horses on the ground, which smelled terrible after a few days—even worse than the gunpowder.

"And it never seemed to settle anything. Because in a year or two they'd be back again for another battle and ruin the landscape some more.

"Well, I had never seen any of these battles myself, being a young wasp. Nevertheless I had heard a whole lot about

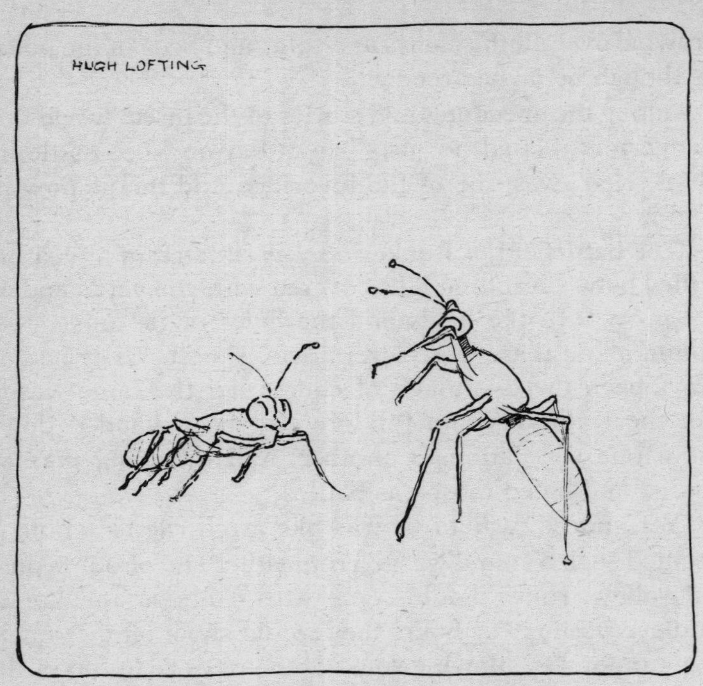

" 'How do you know?' I asked"

them from older relatives. But one evening, just as we were putting the finishing touches to a brand-new nest, one of my uncles came in and said, 'Listen, you can all save yourselves the trouble of any further work on that job. There's going to be another battle.'

" 'How do you know?' I asked.

" 'Because,' says he, 'I've seen them getting ready, up there at the mouth of the valley, digging in the big cannons on the hillside just the way they did last time. And that same general is there who was in charge last time too,

General Blohardi, as they call him. His battles are always more messy than anybody else's.'

"Well, when I heard this I was fired with a great ardor to do something. Our nest, which we had just finished, should be, I felt, defended. The next day I went out to look over the situation. I flew down to the south end of the valley, and there, sure enough, were men in red coats digging in enormous cannon and making no end of a mess. Behind them as far as the eye could reach were tents and tethered horses and ammunition wagons and all the other paraphernalia of war.

"I went down to the other end of the valley and there was another army doing the same thing. When they were ready the two armies would come forward into the middle of the valley and fight out their silly battle.

"On the following day, early in the morning, we were awakened by a great blowing of bugles and beating of drums. Still hopeful that I might do something on behalf of my fellow wasps—though I had no idea what it could be—I left the nest and started out again to reconnoiter.

"About the center of the valley, up on the hills to one side, there was an especially high knoll. On this I saw the figures of horses and men. I flew over nearer to investigate.

"I found a group of very grandly dressed persons gathered about a man on horseback who seemed to be a highly important individual. He kept looking through field glasses this way and that, up and down the valley. Messengers were arriving and departing all the time, bringing him news from every quarter.

"I decided that this must be the famous General Blohardi himself. Now about these names I am not very

"His long red mustache puffed out like the whiskers on a walrus"

certain. They were names that we wasps gave and they may not be the right names at all. We called him General Blohardi because he was always blowing so hard through his long red mustache, which puffed out before him when he spoke, like the whiskers on a walrus. The two armies were the Smithereenians and the Bombasteronians—but those also may not be the regular names. General Blohardi was the field marshal of the Bombasteronian army.

"It was clear that the general had come up to this high

point so he could get a good view of the fight—also no doubt because he wanted to stay in a safe place himself. Evidently, from the way in which he kept blowing out his mustaches, he expected a very fine battle—one of his messiest. Before he would be done with our beautiful valley it would be just a howling wilderness full of broken trees, dead and wounded men, and maimed horses.

"I felt so furious as I watched him there, snapping out his pompous orders, I was ready to do anything. Yet what could I do? I was such a tiny creature. A mere wasp!

"Presently a bugle blew far down the valley. It was followed almost immediately by the roar of cannon. All the horses moved restlessly and the general and his officers leaned forward in their saddles to see the show.

"The battle had begun!

"As I noticed the horses move restlessly at the first roar of the cannon an idea came to me. It would be no use my going and stinging General Blohardi on the nose—though I would dearly have loved to do so. But if I stung his horse I might possibly accomplish something. The animal was a lovely steed, cream-colored, groomed to perfection, high-spirited and as nervous as a witch.

"Well—no sooner thought than done. I hopped onto the horse behind the general and stung the poor fellow in the flank. It was a dirty trick to play on the horse and I wanted to apologize to him afterwards, but he was much too far away.

"The results were instantaneous and astounding. The horse gave one bound and shot off down the hill with me and the general, as fast as he could go. By this time the armies were on their way toward the center of the valley. I had to cling for all I was worth not to be blown off by the

"The horse gave one bound"

rushing wind. I crawled along his flank and stung him in another place. Then he went faster still.

"When we reached the level in the bottom of the valley where the cavalry were already charging, I feared he might turn and join the other horses. So I stung him a third time. At this, he put on such speed that I was blown off and had to fly behind—where I had great difficulty keeping up with him. On and on and on he went, straight across the flat and up the other slope.

"Now, as I have said, Blohardi was the commander in

chief of the Bombasteronians. And when the cavalry of that army saw their famous general in full flight, leaving the battlefield at goodness knows how many miles an hour, it completely disheartened and demoralized them. They, too, took to their heels. And that was the end of the battle.

"The general of the Smithereenians got no end of decorations and honors for the victory of Bunkerloo. But," Tangerine ended modestly, "it was, as you see, really I who had won the battle . . . Now I'd like a little more marmalade, please."

· The Fourth Chapter ·

DOMESTIC INSECTS

I HAVE never seen poor Dab-Dab in such a state of fuss and annoyance in my life as she was these days.

"It was bad enough," she said to me one evening on the brink of tears, "when the Doctor used to fill the house with lame badgers and rheumatic field mice. But this is a thousand times worse. What's the use of my trying to keep the house clean when he does nothing but ruin and smother it with bugs and insects. The latest is he is making friends with the spiders in the cellar. Their webs, he says, mustn't be brushed away. For years I've been working to get the place free of cockroaches; and last night he was hunting everywhere with a lantern.

" 'Surely, Dab-Dab,' says he, 'we have *some* cockroaches?'

" 'Surely we have *not,*' says I. 'It took me a long time to get rid of them, but I succeeded at last. Not one roach will you find in my kitchen!'

" 'Dear, dear!' he mutters. 'I wanted one to talk to. I wonder if Matthew Mugg would have any in his house!'

"And off he goes to get that good-for-nothing Matthew to

" 'Surely, Dab-Dab,' said he, 'we have *some* cockroaches!' "

supply him with cockroaches. Of course once they get back in the house they'll breed and be all over the place again in no time; and all because he wants to talk to them, mind you. And who cares, I'd like to know, what a cockroach might have to say—or a spider, either? That's the worst of the Doctor, he has no—er—sense in some things."

"Well, Dab-Dab," said I consolingly, "this present study may not last very long, you know. There are so many fresh branches of natural history continually claiming his attention, it's quite possible that by next week he will be off on a

" 'Well,' said she, 'happily, Jip gave him very little encouragement' "

new departure entirely and you will be able to get your house in order again."

Dab-Dab shook her head sadly.

"I haven't much hope," said she. "There's a whole lot of different bugs he has still to listen to, as he calls it. Why, do you know, Tommy, what I heard him saying the other day?"

The housekeeper dropped her voice and glanced guiltily over her shoulder.

"I heard him asking Jip if he thought *fleas* could talk!"

"And what did Jip say?" I asked. I confess I could not help smiling at the look of horror on her face.

"Well," said she, "happily, Jip gave him very little encouragement. 'Fleas?' he growled. 'All they can do is bite. Don't have anything to do with 'em, Doctor. They're a dirty lot!' "

· The Fifth Chapter ·

THE WATER BEETLE

THE next experiment that we made in insect language was entirely different from any we had conducted so far and turned out to be one of the most successful. It was much more like our research work in shellfish speech than anything we had done so far. By perfecting and extending the apparatus we had used for aquatic and marine creatures we managed to establish very good contact with the water beetle. His conversation was quite plain and John Dolittle seemed to have very little difficulty in following what he was trying to say. This surprised me somewhat because he never seemed to stay still an instant, but was forever flying and shooting around the glass jar in which the Doctor kept him; now swimming freely in the clear water; now burrowing into the mud at the bottom; now perching on a water plant and polishing his nose with his front feet.

After the Doctor had conveyed to him what it was he wanted to know, he told us the following story:

"It is about our traveling you want to know, huh! Well, of

"He was forever shooting around this glass jar

course being able to swim and walk and fly, we do a good deal of touring. But this, I fancy, is not what *you* would call traveling. It is all short-distance work, though much of it is very interesting. We water beetles are very fortunate, I suppose, since there are hardly any animals that care to fight with us. The big pickerel and pike are about our only dangerous enemies; they have to be quite hungry before they will consider us good eating. I have occasionally had to leave the water and take to my wings when being chased by these ferocious fish and have even had to leave one pond or stream altogether, when they had become too numerous, and seek other water homes. But those times were, happily, rare. The first occasion that I took a really big journey was on the foot of a duck."

At this point the Doctor stopped the proceedings, fearing that he might not have heard aright.

"A journey on the foot of a duck?" he asked. "I don't quite understand. Would you mind explaining that?"

"Certainly," said the water beetle. "It is quite simple. You see, when we are not out swimming freely in the water in search of food we usually work our way down into the mud below, to the depth of, say, half an inch to two inches. This often enables us to hide away from the fish of prey who cannot dig for us. We are really very safe. Few water beetles ever fall victims to their enemies in their own element.

"But I and a friend of mine were once carried off from our native pond and transported an enormous distance—well, as I told you, on the foot of a duck. Our pond was way out in a lonely, marshy stretch of country where few people ever came. Those who did, came in the fall and winter to shoot ducks. Of ducks there we had plenty, also every other kind of wildfowl—snipe, geese, plovers, redshanks, curlews, herons, and whatnot. Even of these we water beetles were not afraid. We only had to burrow into the mud an inch or two and we were usually safe. But we didn't like the ducks. They used to come in from the sea and descend upon our pond in thousands at nighttime. And such a quacking and a stirring up of the water they made! They'd gobble up the weeds like gluttons and any small fish such as fresh water shrimps or other pond creatures they could lay hold of.

"One night I and a friend of mine were swimming around peacefully and suddenly he said, 'Look out! Ducks! I saw their shadow crossing the moon. Get down into the mud.'

"I took his advice right away. Together we burrowed into the mud without any further argument. The water over us was barely above three inches deep. In hundreds the ducks descended. Even below the surface of the mud we could hear their commotion and clatter. How they paddled and stirred around!

"Then suddenly: *Bang! Bang!*

"Some sportsmen nearby who had laid in wait for them had opened fire. We had heard this happen before; and we were always glad because the sportsmen drove the ducks away and left our pond in peace.

"For what happened next I have to rely on another water beetle who returned to our pond just at the moment when the sportsmen opened fire. Because, of course, I and my friend, being below the mud, could neither see nor hear anything.

"Ducks were dropping in all directions, splashing into the water—some wounded, some killed outright. It was a terrible slaughter. Some of them who had been cruising in the water near where we were rose instantly on the first shot and were killed a few feet above the surface of the pond. But one, it seems, was sort of late in getting up and that very likely saved his life; for while the sportsmen were reloading their guns he got away. The water, as I have told you, was very shallow just there and he was actually standing on the muddy bottom, wading. As he gave a jump to take off, his broad, webbed feet sank into the mud an inch

"He took to the air with a cake of mud on each foot"

or two. And he took to the air with a big cake of mud on each foot. I and my friend were in those cakes of mud.

"Now this species of duck, which was not an ordinary or common one, was apparently about to make its migration flight that night. The flight was, in fact, already in progress and the flock had stopped at our pond to feed on its way. With this alarm the remainder of the ducks at once headed out to sea.

"As for me, I had no idea for some moments of what had happened. And I could not communicate with my friend because he was on one of the duck's feet and I was on the other. But with the rushing of the wind and the quick drying of the mud, I soon realized that something very unusual was taking place. Before the mud dried entirely hard I burrowed my way to the surface of the cake and took a peep outside.

"I saw then that I was thousands of feet up in the air. And from the shimmer of starlight on wide water far, far below, I gathered that I was being carried over the sea. I confess I was scared. For a moment I had a notion to scramble out and take to my own wings. But the duck's enormous speed warned me that we were probably already many miles from land. Even supposing that I could tell which direction to go back in—I knew, of course, nothing of this big-scale navigation such as birds use in their long flights—I was afraid of the powerful winds that were rushing by us. In strength, my own wings were not made for doing battle with such conditions.

"No, it was clear that whether I liked it or not I had got to stay where I was for the present. It was certainly a strange accident to happen to anyone, to be picked out of his native haunts and carried across the sea to foreign lands on the foot of a duck!

"My great fear now was that the mud might drop off in midflight and go splashing down into the sea with me inside it. As a precaution against this I kept near to the hole I had made to look out through, so that I would be able to take to my own wings if necessary. Through this I nearly froze to death. The rushing of the cold air was terrific. My goodness, what a speed that duck kept up! I drew back into the inner shelter of the mud cake. I knew that so long as I could hear that droning, deafening whirl of the duck's wings I was still attached to my flying steed.

"Pretty soon now the mud got so hard that any further drilling through it was out of the question. But as I had already made myself a little chamber runway by turning around and around in it before it hardened completely, I was quite comfortable so far as that was concerned. I remember as I peeped out of my little window—nearly freezing my nose—I saw the dawn come up over the sea. It was a wonderful sight; at that great height the sun's rays reached us long before they touched the sea. The ocean stretched, gloomy, black, and limitless, beneath us, while the many-colored eastern sky glowed and reflected on the myriads of ducks who were flying along beside mine, necks outstretched, glowing golden and pink—all headed toward their new homeland.

"I was glad to see the day arrive for more reasons than one. It made the air warmer. And I could now see if any land were to come in sight.

"I was still very anxious about getting dropped into the sea. Once we got over land of any kind I would feel happier. The ducks started honking to one another as they saw the dawn. It almost seemed as though they were exchanging signals as conversation of some kind because I suddenly saw that they somewhat changed direction following a leader, a single duck, who flew at the head of the V-shaped flock."

· The Sixth Chapter ·

THE END OF THE JOURNEY

THE change of direction caused me to wonder why the leader of the flock had made it. I crept to the edge of my hole in the mud cake and craned my neck out as far as I dared so as to get a view ahead.

"And there, a little to the left of where the sun was rising, lay a low line of something sitting on the sea. The morning rays made it glow like molten silver at one end; and at the other, where the light had not yet reached, it was dark and black.

"Land! The flock was heading for it. Would they rest there or just take their bearings and pass on? My bird, at all events, didn't seem in need of a rest. After a whole night's going he seemed as fresh as a fiddle and was whacking away with those great wings of his, as though he had only just started.

"It didn't take the leader long to make up his mind. He came sailing over the low-lying islands with his gallant band. He circled a couple of times while the others hung

"To the left of where the sun was rising lay a low line of something sitting on the sea"

back, quacking. Then he shot off again, headed once more for the open sea where no land bounded the horizon.

"Goodness! I thought. How long is this life going to last?

"But now the sea was all lit up and bright with the risen sun. It seemed to put new heart into the fliers, for their quacking and honking broke out louder than ever as they swung off in the new direction after their leader. I began to wonder how many other small creatures like myself had thus shared the flight of migrating birds. It was certainly an extraordinary experience. Also, I wondered how my friend was getting on in the mud on my duck's other foot.

"I had a notion to crawl forth and go and see. But the moment I found my nose out of the hole in my mud cake I realized that that would be madness. The rush of the air past the duck's stomach was enough to blow your eyes out, and besides, if the bird should feel me creeping up one leg and down the other it was quite likely he would scratch his feet together to knock me off. I decided I had better not try to get into communication with my friend till we were on solid ground. Indeed it was lucky that the duck kept his feet tucked well back against his feathers. It was that, I am sure, that kept the mud from falling off and sending me to a watery grave in the wide sea below.

"Well, at last we came to the land the ducks were making for. We sighted it on the evening of that second day. Great rocky headlands jutted out into the ocean, some high, some low. The chief of the flock led his followers over it and then swung to the left. I imagine it was southward. It looked as though he now meant to follow the shoreline down till he came to the exact region he was seeking.

"Anyway, I felt more at ease. If I got dropped now—the ducks still maintained a considerable height—I could crawl out of the mud cake before it struck the earth and on my own wings land safely in some sort of territory where I'd stand a chance of surviving.

"Not only did the ducks keep up at a great height, but they also kept up their perfectly incredible speed. And very soon I noticed that the climate was changing considerably. It got warmer and warmer. I became quite lively. And now I could look out of the hole in the mud cake and watch the changing landscape below without any fear of getting frostbitten. And my gracious, how that landscape did change! One moment we were over flat, marshy fenland that stretched away as though it would never end; and the next it was mountains, range upon range, with here and there a glimpse of the sea, where great crested capes stretched out into the surf, and you could see the waves breaking against the feet of high cliffs.

"The greenery also changed—now sparse, nothing but scrub shrubbery, which barely covered the big expanse of smooth rock. Then came parklands where I could spy deer grazing and still larger creatures. And finally we flew over dense, deep jungles where the trees were so thick and close-packed you felt you would alight on a velvet carpet if you just sailed down and landed.

"At length some signal seemed to be sent back from the leader up ahead. Because all the flock stopped and started circling and eddying away in the wildest manner. We had arrived over a wide, wide bay on the shoreline. The coast seemed low, and behind it were many ponds and lagoons. I could tell from the dizzy singing in my ears that my duck was descending—like the rest—in widening circles to the flat marshlands they had come so far to seek."

· The Seventh Chapter ·
THE COLONY OF EXILES

YOU can imagine how glad I was to reach real solid ground again. The duck's plump body came to rest in the marshy ground without noise or fuss. It seemed almost as though he had merely flown from one pond to another, instead of crossing those leagues of wild ocean and thousands of miles of land. He just shook himself, grunted, and began to look about for something to eat.

"Of course as soon as he moved the cakes of dry English earth that had clung to his feet all the way came off in the wet mud of this foreign land. And poor little me with them. Oh, such a relief! At once I crept out of the hole and swam forth into the cool, oozy mud of the lagoon. I was hungry myself. I too bustled around to raise some food.

"But for me the territory was new. The ducks had been there before. It was their winter home. They knew all the grasses, all the shellfish, all the water life fit to eat. But I! I suddenly found myself swimming about in a tropical lagoon full of large strange enemies and small new creatures that might be food or might be poison.

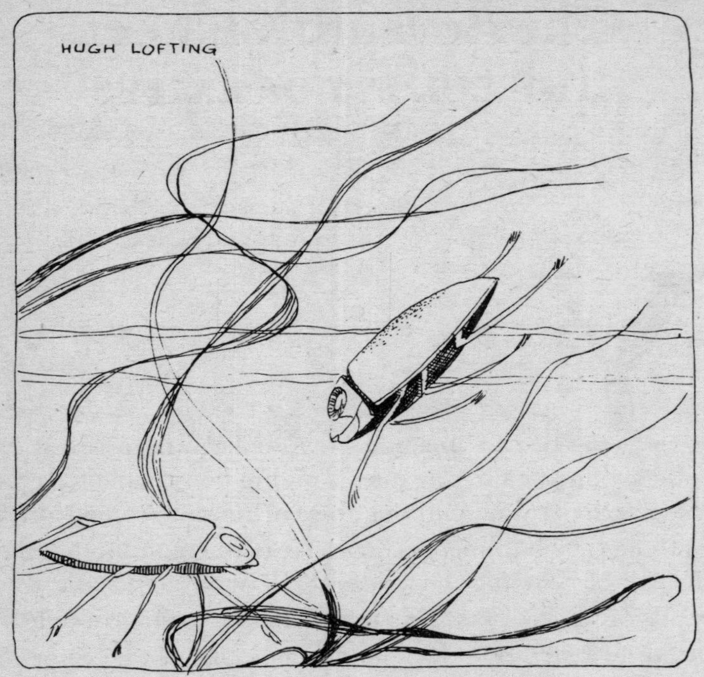

"I maneuvered about him for a while"

"I swam for hours before I dared act. I was taking no chances after coming through that long journey of danger and adventure. At last I met an insect that looked familiar. I maneuvered about him for a while. The water was kind of muddy, stirred up from the paddling and wading of the ducks. Then I recognized him. It was my friend who had made the journey on the other foot of the same duck. We almost fell on one another's necks.

" 'Tell me,' I said, 'where can I find something to eat. These waters contain nothing but strange sights for me.'

"He laughed. 'Why,' said he, 'I've just had the grandest meal of my life—fish eggs in plenty. Come with me. I'll show you.'

" 'But what about those dangerous-looking fellows?' I said. 'It seems to me we're surrounded by nothing but enemies.'

"He glanced back at me and chuckled over his shoulder as he led the way. 'Don't forget that we are just as strange to these fellows here as they are to us,' said he. 'They don't know what to make of us—as yet, anyway. They're just as scared of us as you are of them.'

"Now pond life is, as you probably know, a very strenuous business. All kinds of creatures—fish, beetles, worms, salamanders—every species has its enemies. And if you want to live to a ripe old age, you've got to look out. And so as I followed my friend, and everything from great pike to ferocious-looking turtles came up and glowered at us through murky waters, you may be sure I felt far from comfortable.

"But in a little while I realized that many of the larger species who in our own waters would not have hesitated to attack us, here were by no means so bold and seemed almost, as my friend had said, to be scared of us.

"After we had had something to eat we crept out of the lagoon onto the muddy bank to take a look around. The ducks were still feeding. All kinds of other waterfowl too, many of which I had never seen before. Some of them were quite curious and beautiful: long-legged fellows like great cranes with scarlet bills and wings; flat-headed smaller kinds like snipe, built for speed with tiny beaks and mincing gait; geese and wild swans of various sorts;

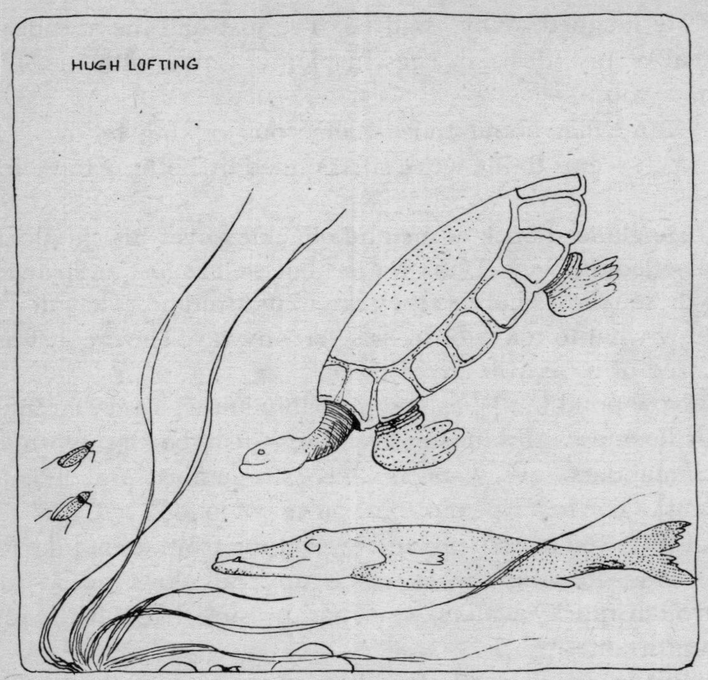

"Came up and glowered at us through murky waters"

and great big-mouthed pelicans that dove for fish with a mighty splash and gobbled up their prey by the bushel.

"It seemed a regular paradise for birds, no sign of human habitation in sight. On one side, lagoon after lagoon led outward to the sea; on the other, flat marshland lay between us and the mountains.

" 'This,' I said to my friend, 'seems like a very nice place we have come to.'

" 'Yes,' he replied. 'I don't think we have done so badly. I wonder if any more of our kind ever came to these parts.'

" 'You never can tell,' said I. 'Let's look around and find out.'

"So off we swam together down the lagoon to see if we could find any others of our own kin who had been exiled on these foreign shores.

"After about an hour's search—the lagoon was several miles long and had many lesser lagoons running off it in every direction—we came upon one or two solitary specimens of our own kind. They were very glad to see us and at once asked for news of the homeland. We told them what we could. But the information they could give us was much more important. They had been here some time and had already gotten acclimatized. Familiar as they were with the dangers and the advantages of the waters, they told us what parts to avoid and where the best feeding was to be found. The temperature of the water was of course, generally speaking, very much higher than that of our native haunts. But they had discovered that by seeking certain very shallow places at night, when the wind regularly blew down from the mountains, cooler territory could always be found. While by day special spots where rocky creeks ran into the lagoon afforded some relief from the tropical heat.

"Well, with these few fellow beetles whom we discovered here (it seems they had probably been imported the same way that we had) we formed a regular little colony. That is, it was little to begin with. But very soon we had large families of young ones growing up and after a few months we felt that we formed quite an important species in the pond life of that region. That, I think, is about all I have to tell you of how I went abroad."

"The beetles in my native pond turned out to do me honor"

"Oh, but listen," said the Doctor, "you haven't told us yet how you got back here."

"That is quite simple," said the beetle. "I came back by the same means as I went out: on the feet of some water-fowl. Only on the return journey I am not so sure what kind of bird it was that carried me. As soon as I realized I had been returned to England it did not take me long to find my way back to my own particular pond. My case was, of course, peculiar. I know now that quite a few small water creatures get carried abroad—sometimes in egg form only—in that same way. But it is exceptionally rare, I fancy, for one individual to get back to the waters that he started from. I was given quite a wonderful reception. The beetles in my native pond turned out to do me honor. And I felt like a great traveler who had done something wonderful."

· The Eighth Chapter ·

A LIFETIME OF TWENTY-FOUR HOURS

AT the conclusion of the water beetle's story the Doctor, as he had done with the other insects, put many questions to him by which he hoped to get some practical natural history out of his strange tale.

"Could you describe to me," he asked, "the appearance of that duck that carried you abroad on his feet?"

Thereupon the beetle told us what he remembered of this species of wildfowl that regularly visited his native pond—a splash of pink on the cheeks, gray wing feathers, etc.

When he had done the Doctor muttered to me, "It wasn't a duck at all, Stubbins, I fancy. Sounds to me much more like one of the rarer geese. I had suspected that the feet of a duck could hardly accommodate a cake of mud big enough to carry him without discomfort. I think I know the bird he means. Only visits certain parts of England in the early fall. Now we'll see what we can find out about the geography of the trip."

John Dolittle then asked him certain things about the

winds on the voyage, the appearance of the islands the birds flew over, and of the coastline down which they traveled before they reached their final destination.

The beetle's answers to these questions seemed to please the Doctor a great deal. For before they were ended he suddenly grabbed me by the arm and said, "It's northern Brazil, Stubbins. I'm sure of it. This is quite valuable information. I had often wondered how that species got out on to the American side. Everything points to it: the bird that carried him, the islands, the coastline—everything. This will complete a very important chapter in my pamphlet. My gracious, if I could only train some of those insects to note the things I wanted to know! The whole trouble is, of course, that they only observe those things that are of value to themselves. But maybe—er—perhaps later on . . ."

He paused, silent.

"Why, Doctor," I laughed, "are you going to make naturalists out of beetles now?"

"If I only could," he replied quite seriously. "For mark you, Stubbins, there are many things in natural history that *only* a beetle gets the chance to observe."

After he had thanked the water beetle for his kind services we carried him down to the old fishpond at the bottom of the garden and let him go.

Our next experiments in insect language were extremely interesting. They were concerned with a family of flies that, John Dolittle told me, were called the *Ephemera.* These creatures lived their whole life cycle within the space of one day.

"I am very anxious, Stubbins," said he as we were beginning, "to learn what it feels like to be born, live a whole life, and pass away—all in twenty-four hours. A dog lives from ten to twenty years; men from sixty to ninety; the mountains last many thousands before they crumble away. But these little fellows are content to pack all the joys and experiences of life into twenty-four hours. Some of their philosophy, their observations, should, I think, be very valuable to us."

And so with a pale, gossamerlike, green fly on the platform of our most delicate listening machine, we set to work. The poor little creature was already middle-aged because he had been born early that morning and it was now two o'clock in the afternoon. He seemed very frail, and one could easily understand that so unrobust a constitution wasn't made to last very long.

We worked on him for half an hour and our results were very meager. He had things to say, we felt sure. But it was a language new to us. Clearly anyone who has to pack his whole life into one day must talk very fast. We soon got the impression that he was really pouring out hundreds of words a second. Only we weren't catching them quickly enough.

"Look here, Stubbins," said the Doctor, "we are being entirely heartless. We can't let this poor fellow spend more than half an hour talking to us. Why, half an hour out of his life is a forty-eighth part of the whole. That would be nearly eighteen months for us. Imagine anyone talking to you for a year and a half without stopping! Let him go at once. We must do this on a different system. We will catch several singly and only keep them in the apparatus for five minutes at a time. If we are swift enough with our note-taking, we shall perhaps be able to gather a little from what each one says and piece it all together afterwards and make something of it."

And so by catching a number of ephemera and listening to each for a very short period we went on with our experiment.

The results of our labors after ten or twelve days were really quite good—in the circumstances. By very exhaustive and continuous work we learned to follow the extraordinary language of this species with fair ease.

This chapter in the book which John Dolittle later completed on insect language was perhaps the most interesting in the whole work. For not only had this species a tremendously swift and condensed way of speaking, but its powers of observation were correspondingly quick. In any life that lasts only twenty-four hours your impressions of this world must of course be taken in at great speed. More than that, these impressions proved to be very original—quite different from those of any class of insects which we had so far studied. I think it is safe to say that the ephemera wasted less time in forming their opinions and making their decisions than any other class of animal life.

· The Ninth Chapter ·

DAB-DAB'S VIEWS ON INSECT LIFE

A FORTNIGHT later we were all gathered around the kitchen fire after supper. I had been working pretty hard at my secretarial duties and the Doctor had insisted that I take an evening off. But he of course, who never seemed to take, or need, a rest, was busy outside in his sheds on some new phase of his studies in insect language.

"I wonder," said Chee-Chee looking dreamily into the fire, "how much longer he is going to occupy himself with these miserable bugs. Seems to me a sort of a dull study. It should be getting near the time for him to take a voyage, don't you think so, Tommy?"

"Well," I said, "let us see: How long is it since he went on one?"

"Five months, one week, and three days," said Chee-Chee.

"We got back on the twenty-third of October—in the afternoon," Polynesia put in.

"Dear me! How precise you are!" said I. "I suppose you

two old globe-trotters are hankering to be off again. Homesick for Africa?"

"Well, not necessarily Africa," said Chee-Chee. "But I admit I would like to see him get started on something more exciting than listening to cockroaches."

"The next voyage he goes on," said Gub-Gub, "he must take me with him. I haven't been abroad since he visited the Land of the Monkeys, and the Kingdom of the Jolliginki. It's my turn to go. Besides, I need it in my education. There must be a chapter, in my *Encyclopedia of Food,* on African cooking."

"Humph!" grunted Dab-Dab, who was clearing away the dishes from the table behind us. "I don't know where the funds are coming from if he does go on another voyage. There is precious little left in the money box."

"Thirteen pounds, nine shillings, and twopence-halfpenny," put in Too-Too the accountant,"—and the baker's bill for last month not paid yet."

"If you think you are going to get the Doctor to drop bug language for a long while yet, you are sadly mistaken," said Dab-Dab. "What do you think he was talking of last night?"

"I've no idea, Dab-Dab," said I.

"Well," continued the housekeeper in a weary voice, "he mentioned—just mentioned in passing, you know—that he thought it would be a good thing if he did something for . . . for"—she seemed to have great difficulty in bringing herself to pronounce the fatal word—"for *houseflies!*"

"For houseflies!" I cried. "What on earth was he going to do for them?"

"The Lord only knows," groaned Dab-Dab, her voice full of patient weariness. "That's what I said to him: 'Doctor,' I said, 'what in the name of goodness can you do for house-flies, the greatest pest on earth—creatures that do nothing but carry disease and ruin good food?'

" 'Well,' says he, 'that's just the point, Dab-Dab. The houseflies have no friends. Perhaps if some naturalist, and a really great naturalist, Dab-Dab—one who could look far, far ahead—were to take up their cause and see what could be done for them, they could be made into friends for the rest of creation instead of enemies. I would like, as an experiment, to start a Country House for Houseflies. I think it might lead to some very interesting results.'

"There," Dab-Dab continued, "I flew right off the handle. I admit I don't often lose my temper"—she swept some cheese-crumbs savagely off a chair seat with her right wing —" 'Doctor,' I said, 'that is the last straw. You've had a home for lost dogs; a rat-and-mouse club; a squirrel's hotel; a rabbit's apartment house, and heaven only knows how many more crazy notions. But the idea, *the very idea,* of a *Country House for Houseflies!*— well, that to my way of thinking is about the end. Can't you see,' I said, 'that this encouragement of other animal species—without more er—er—discrimination, I think you call it—will lead to the ruin and destruction of your own kind and mine? Some creatures just can't be made friends of. Encourage the houseflies and Man disappears.'

" 'Well,' he said, 'I've been talking to them. And I must confess there is a good deal to be said on their side. After all, they have their rights.'

" 'Not with me, they haven't,' said I. 'They are a nuisance and a pest and cannot be treated as anything else.' Such a man! What can one do with him?"

"Still," put in Gub-Gub, "it *is* a wonderful idea—a Country House for Houseflies! I suppose they would have a boy-swat for swatting boys who came in and disturbed them—the same as people have a fly-swat to kill flies . . . And maybe have papers full of sticky goo near the door, in which people would get tangled up and stuck if they invaded the premises . . . It's quite an idea. I'd like to see it started."

"You'd like to see it started, would you?" screamed Dab-Dab, rushing at poor Gub-Gub with outstretched neck as though she meant to skewer him against the wainscote. "You haven't the wits of a cockroach yourself. You get started on your way to bed at once—or I'll get out the frying pan as a pig-swat."

Gub-Gub retired into a corner.

"Just the same, it's a good idea," he muttered to Too-Too as he settled down where the irate housekeeper couldn't see him.

I am glad to say that the Doctor did not, as a matter of fact, attempt this wild plan for the encouragement of houseflies. Heaven only knows what would have happened if he had.

"There were other insect species that you thought of investigating, were there not?" I asked, hoping to sidetrack him away from the houseflies, which to me sounded like a rather hopeless direction.

"Oh, yes, yes—to be sure, to be sure," said he hurriedly. "I've only just started. There are the moths and butterflies. From them I hope to learn a great deal. It is hardly the right season yet for the natural hatching out of butterflies and moths. But I have been working on my artificial

" 'Just the same, it's a good idea,' he muttered to Too-Too"

incubators. We have a splendid supply of chrysalises. I think I can turn out in the next few weeks about any kind of moth and butterfly I want—that is, of those varieties that are naturally found in these parts."

· The Tenth Chapter ·

THE GIANT MOTHS

THE following evening before the Doctor returned to his sheds outside the house, Chee-Chee broached the subject of a voyage. This, rather to our surprise, had the effect of keeping the Doctor in the fireside circle for several hours later than was his custom.

"Well, Chee-Chee," said he, "I'd like to take a voyage—it's quite a while since I went abroad—but you see, there is so much work yet to be done on insect language right here at home. I never believe in leaving anything unfinished—if I can possibly avoid it."

"Yes, but listen, Doctor," said Polynesia. "You will learn a whole lot more about insects and their languages abroad. It never seemed to me that traveling ever interrupted *your* studies. On the contrary, the farther you were from home and the more difficult the conditions that faced you, the more you got done—so far as I could see."

"Humph!" muttered the Doctor. "That's quite a compliment, Polynesia; I wonder if it's true."

"In any case, Doctor," said I, "it's a long while since you

were on a voyage. And you know one does miss a lot if he does not go abroad every so often."

"That's so," said he. "That's true enough. But then the trouble is: where to go? You know, Stubbins, I'm afraid that in my old age I've gotten very hard to please in the matter of travel. All the big and important exploration has been done. Why should I worry about mapping the details of the smaller geography when there is the languages of the insects, with all they may have to tell us, still a secret to mankind?

"Yes, but, Doctor," I said, "abroad, as Polynesia suggests, you might accomplish still better results in your studies."

"Abroad!" John Dolittle's voice sounded, to my surprise, almost contemptuous. He walked over to the window and threw back the curtains. The light of the full moon poured into the room.

"Stubbins," he said suddenly in a strange, intense voice, "if I could get to the moon! That would be worthwhile! Columbus discovered a new half of our own planet. All alone he did it, pitting his opinion against the rest of the world. It was a great feat. The days of big discovery are gone by. But if I could reach the moon, then I could feel I was truly great—a greater explorer than Columbus. The moon—how beautiful she looks!"

"Lord save us," whispered Polynesia. "What's come over the good man?"

"Humph!" muttered Bumpo. "It seems to me the Doctor is just talking happy-go-foolish, as it were. The moon! How could he get there?"

"It is not such a wild notion, Stubbins," said John Dolittle, leaving the window and appealing to me with outstretched hands. "Someone will do it—someday. It stands to reason. What a step it would be! The naturalist who first reached the moon! Ah! He will be the one to make strides in science—maybe to give all investigation a new start."

"Listen, Doctor," said Polynesia, evidently anxious to call him back to earth and practical matters, "we haven't had a story from you in ever so long. How would it be if you told us one tonight?"

"Story . . . story?" mumbled the Doctor, in a faraway sort of voice. "My head is too full of problems. Get one of the family to tell one. Tell one yourself, Polynesia—you know plenty. Or Chee-Chee—yours are always worth hearing."

"It would be better, Doctor," said Chee-Chee, "if you told us one. It isn't often, lately, that you've been home evenings."

"Not tonight, Chee-Chee. Not tonight," said John Dolittle, going back to the window and looking up again at the moon. "I told you: My head is full of problems—and moths."

"What do you mean, your head is full of moths, Doctor?" asked Dab-Dab in rather an alarmed voice.

"Oh," said the Doctor, laughing, "I just meant the study of moth language—and its problems. I've been at it now for several days and nights, and my head is full of it."

"You should take a rest," said Chee-Chee. "A voyage would be a fine change for you—and all of us."

Now the Doctor had put in a good deal of time on the moths already, I knew, without my assistance. I was naturally keen to hear if he had made any special discoveries. I had become so much a part of his research work that I felt almost a bit jealous now if he went off on his own and left me out.

"Had you heard anything of unusual importance, Doctor," I asked, "in your work recently with the moths?"

"Well, yes," he said. "I hatched out one of the hawks last night—a beautiful specimen. I put her—she was a lady moth—in a glass dome with a small light in it on the windowsill. Great numbers of gentlemen hawks came to call on her. How they gathered so suddenly when their species has never been seen within a hundred miles of here, goodness only knows. I caught a few and experimented with them in the listening machines. And—er . . ."

He hesitated a moment with a puzzled look on his face.

"Well," I asked, "what did they tell you?"

"It was most extraordinary," he said at length. "They didn't seem to want to let me know where they came from, nor how they had found their way here. Quite mysterious. So I gave up that line of inquiry and asked for general information about their history and traditions. And they told me the wildest story. Perhaps it has no truth in it whatever. But—er—well, you know most of the members of the hawk family are large—that is, for this part of the world. So I got on to the subject of size, and they told me of a race of moths as big—well, I know it sounds crazy—*as big as a house.* I said at once, of course, 'No. It can't be. There's some mistake'—thinking that my scanty knowledge of the language had led me astray. But they insisted. There was a tradition in moth history that somewhere there were moths as big as a house who could lift a ton weight in the air just as though it were a feather. Extraordinary . . . mysterious! The moths are a curious race."

· The Eleventh Chapter ·

OTHO THE PREHISTORIC ARTIST

"OH, WELL, come along now, Doctor," said Chee-Chee, "tell us a story, do."

"Not tonight," John Dolittle repeated. "You tell them one, Chee-Chee."

"All right," said Chee-Chee, "I will. But I am by no means sure this crowd will understand it. I'll tell you one that my grandmother used to tell us—in the jungle—a tale of long, long, long ago."

"Good!" grunted Gub-Gub, coming forward to the table. With the Doctor present he was no longer afraid of Dab-Dab the housekeeper.

"Thousands and thousands and thousands of years ago," Chee-Chee began, "there lived a man. Otho Bludge was his name. He had a whole country to himself, in those far-off days when there weren't so many people in the world. He was an artist, was Otho. He lived to make pictures. Of course there wasn't any paper then and he had to use such materials as he could get. Reindeer horn was what he used mostly. There were plenty of reindeer about. For a pencil he used a stone knife. And with this he would cut his pictures on the flat part of the horn. Sometimes he used rocks, cutting and chiseling into the stone the ideas which occurred to him as worthwhile.

"He had made pictures of deer, fish, butterflies, bison, elephants, and all the creatures that abounded around him. His one great ambition was to make a picture of Man. But Man was scarce. Otho himself was the only specimen in that district. He looked at himself and tried to make a picture of arms and legs. But it wasn't much good. Then he went down to a pool in the stream and tried to draw his own reflection. But he had to lean way over the water to see his image and that was hard, too.

" 'No,' he said, 'I've got to find another creature like myself and make him stand still. Then I'll draw my best picture—a portrait of Man.'

"So he set out hunting. And for days and weeks he wandered over the wide country that he had all to himself and went outside and beyond it in search of a fellow man. But not one could he find. Many interesting new animals he saw—many of whom fought him and chased him across the landscape. Trees too which he had never seen before gave him many fresh ideas for pictures. But Man he could not find. As a matter of fact he had only a very vague idea of ever having seen another human. That was his mother. How she had become separated from him he could not remember—nor how he had managed to survive when left alone.

"So, quite disconsolate and miserable, Otho returned to the place where he usually did his drawings and tried to make his picture of Man without anyone to draw from.

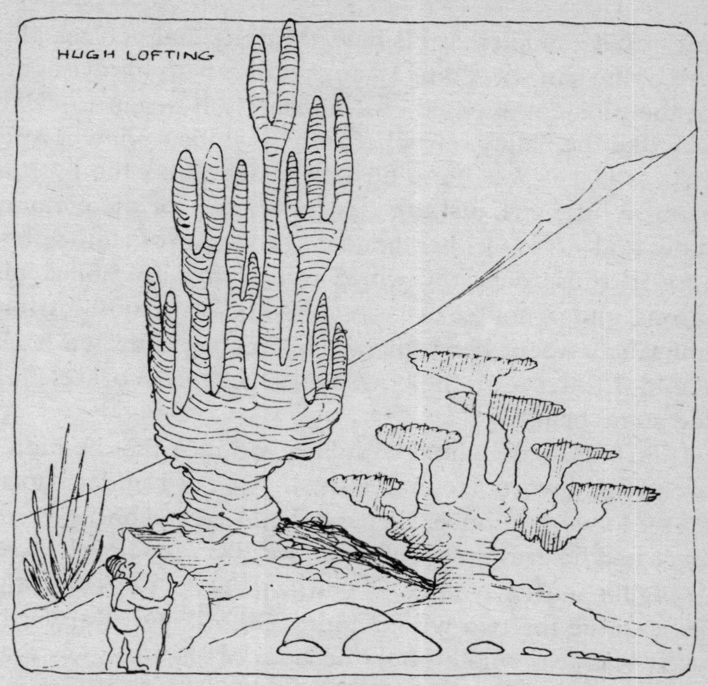

"Trees which he had never seen before gave him ideas"

But it didn't go any better. He could get a leg or an arm or a head to look pretty right, but the whole body didn't seem to fit together at all.

"Then he said to himself aloud—he often talked to himself because he had no one else to talk to—'Oh, how I wish someone would spring out of the ground and stand on that rock over there so I could finish my portrait!'

"And then, what do you think? You could never guess. While he was looking at the rock there he saw a sort of pink fog gathering on top of it. Otho Bludge brushed the back of his hand across his face, thinking that perhaps the glare of the sun was doing strange things with his eyesight. But the pink fog seemed real. Presently it began to clear away like the valley mists before the winds of dawn. And when at last it was gone he saw kneeling on the rock a beautiful little girl, just the way he wanted for the picture, a bow and arrow in her hands. She wore no clothes because in those days the world was frightfully hot at all seasons, and of course skirts and bodices were nothing but a nuisance. About her right wrist, which was drawn back to hold the arrow on the bowstring, she wore a bracelet of blue stone beads.

"Otho was so delighted with his good luck that he didn't dare speak a word. He took a fresh piece of reindeer horn and set to work at once. He carved and carved and carved. Never had he drawn so well in all his life. He knew he was cutting his master picture. The little girl kept perfectly still like a statue for two whole hours. Otho knew afterwards that it was two whole hours because of the shadows that the rocks threw. He used to measure his time by the length of the shadows—having no watch, of course.

"Finally he finished his picture. It was good. He knew it was. He held it off to look at it. But when he glanced back at the rock he noticed that the pink fog was beginning to return."

" 'Good gracious!' said he to himself. 'Can it be that she is going to fade away again?'

"Yes, it seemed like it. The pink fog was growing and she was disappearing. Only a sort of shadow of her now remained. Otho was terribly upset.

" 'Listen,' he called out, 'why are you going away? I've

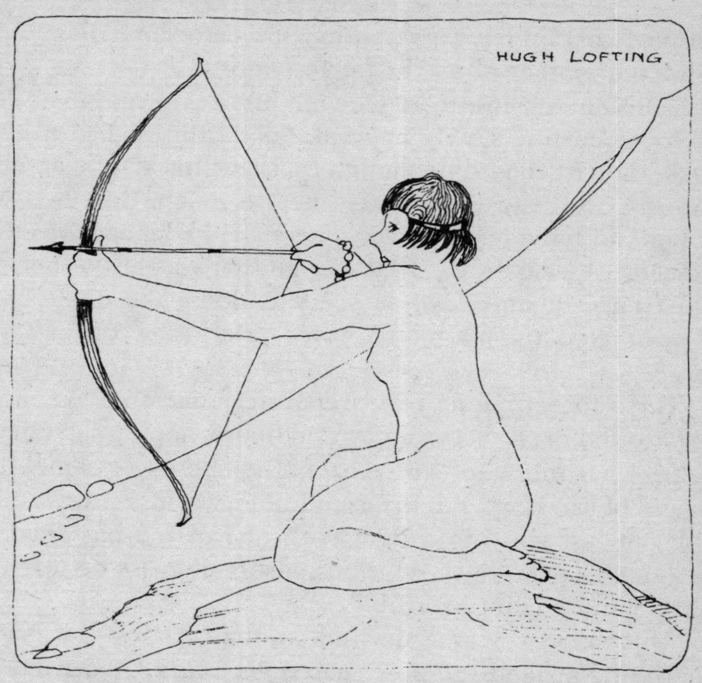

" 'About her right wrist she wore a bracelet of beads' "

got a whole country to myself here—and it's much too big for just one. Why don't you stay and play at housekeeping with me?'

"But she only blushed all over, shook her head, and went on disappearing.

" 'At least you can tell me who you are before you go, can't you?' cried poor Otho, tears coming into his eyes.

"By this time she was nearly gone. Very little remained of her except her voice, which said faintly but musically, 'I am Pippiteepa. I am sorry, but I have to go back into the unseen world. I have a very busy life before me. For I am to be the mother of all the fairies. Farewell!'

"Nothing was now to be seen but just a thin ribbon of the pink fog curling slowly upward. Poor Otho rushed to the rock and clutched it as though by sheer force to keep her in his world where he wanted her so much. But she was gone. And lying on the place where she had stood was the bracelet of blue beads. That was all that was left of her. It must have fallen off while she was doing the disappearance magic. Otho put it on his own wrist and wore it all his life.

"For a long time he was dreadfully miserable, wandering around the rock for hours and hours, hoping she might change her mind and come back. But she never came. It's a kind of sad story, but my grandmother swore it was true. Otho at last got into a fight with one of the big grazing beasts that lived in those times, a sort of cross between a giraffe and a giant lizard.

"This creature came up and wanted to crop the grass that grew around the now sacred rock and Otho tried to drive him off. He got nasty and put up a fight. This kept Otho so busy that it put Pippiteepa out of his mind for the rest of the day. And after a while he went back to making pictures of animals and trees. He carefully kept the portrait he had made of Pippiteepa but never again attempted to make a picture of Man. He went on hoping, always, that some day she would change her mind and come back."

· The Twelfth Chapter ·

THE DAYS BEFORE THERE WAS A MOON

I DON'T know that I have ever seen the Doctor more interested in anything than he seemed to be in this story of Otho Bludge and Pippiteepa.

"Tell me, Chee-Chee," said he, "you say your grandmother told you this story, eh?"

"Yes," Chee-Chee replied, "it was one of her favorite ones. I must have heard her tell it at least a dozen times."

"Humph!" the Doctor grunted, "very curious . . . most peculiar. Did she ever say anything which might give you an idea of when—how long ago—this took place?"

"Well," said Chee-Chee, "of course to me it only seemed like a—er—a legend, I think you call it—something that might have never happened but which was believed by almost everyone."

"But the time?" the Doctor repeated. "You have no idea about when this was supposed to have happened—I mean, anything else that was spoken of as belonging to the same period that might give us some clue?"

"No, I don't think so," Chee-Chee answered, ". . . and

"'I must have heard her tell it at least a dozen times'"

yet, wait—there was something. I remember she always began the story this way: 'In the days before there was a moon,' I could never understand why. It didn't seem to me very important."

Doctor Dolittle almost leapt out of his chair.

"Did your grandmother ever speak of the moon further, Chee-Chee—I mean, anything more than just that?"

"Yes," said Chee-Chee, evidently cudgeling his brain to remember things long past. "It seems that in monkey history, which was of course always a mouth-to-mouth business, there was a belief that the moon was once a part of the earth. And there came a great explosion or something and part of it was shot off into the skies and somehow got stuck there. But how it became round like a ball I could never understand or find anyone who could explain it to me. Because they used to say that the piece of the earth that got shot off was the land where the Pacific Ocean now is and that isn't round at all. But of course the whole thing is by no means certain. Myself, I've always had grave doubts about the truth of any part of the story."

The household was quite delighted over Chee-Chee's story, not only with the entertainment of the tale itself, but because the Doctor became so absorbed in the subject of the moon and the legends of monkey history that he kept us all up till long after midnight.

"You know, Stubbins," he said to me, "no matter how wild this story may sound, it is curiously borne out by several things. For instance, I remember that in my conversation with the giant sea snail he told me of a belief that was firmly held by the older forms of sea life that some such shooting off of part of the earth's surface made the deep ocean and accounted for the moon. Also my geological observations when we were traveling across the floor of the Atlantic certainly pointed to some such violent cleavage—only Chee-Chee says his grandmother spoke of the Pacific Ocean, not the Atlantic. You know it makes me almost want to go back to Africa and question some of the older monkeys there. I might get other versions and more details of this strange story of Otho Bludge and Pippiteepa."

"Well, Doctor," said I, scenting a chance to get him off on a voyage after all—for I felt he sorely needed one—"why not? Last time when you were in Africa, according to Polynesia, anyway, you were so busy with hospital work and getting away from the Jolliginki army that there must have been a great deal of interesting work that had to go undone."

"Oh, but," said he, shaking his head impatiently, "I mustn't be tempted. One would never get anything accomplished by just running off after every attractive idea that pulled one this way or that. I must stick to this insect-language game till I feel I have really done something worthwhile with it. I want to follow up the story the moth told me about a giant species. It is funny, these legends in animal history—the monkeys and the moon: the moths and the giants. There is something in that, I feel sure. The moths are a very mysterious race. I don't believe that one-tenth part of what they do in the general economy of the animal and vegetable kingdoms is appreciated. And imagine what a moth the size of a house might do!"

"But, surely," said I, "if there were such enormous moths flopping about the world, somewhere other people must have seen them. I confess I can hardly believe the story."

"It sounds incredible enough, I know," said he. "But I'm sure that if there were not something in it the story would not exist among the moths."

· The Thirteenth Chapter ·

MEMORIES OF LONG ARROW

FOR me one of the most interesting things in the Doctor's study of insect language was the hatching out of the moths and butterflies from the caterpillar or chrysalis forms. Throughout the previous autumn and part of the winter I had assisted him in the collection of caterpillars and chrysalises and we had a fine stock in the hatching houses. The care of these required considerable knowledge and experience—of which I had not a great deal, though I was always learning. They had to be kept at the right temperature and moisture and each caterpillar had to be fed on a special kind of leaf till he had spun his web and retired into his chrysalis shell. But the Doctor, who had studied butterflies ever since he was a boy of nine, had a positively prodigious knowledge of the subject. He never seemed to make a mistake and in his hands a moth or butterfly could be made to hatch out with just as much ease and comfort as it would in the wild state. In fact, conditions in the Dolittle hatching houses were rather more fortunate for these insects than those of the open, for

"Each caterpillar had to be fed on a special kind of leaf"

they were protected from their enemies, which very frequently in the wild would devour a butterfly or moth almost as soon as it was born into the world.

With some of the rarer and more beautiful moths it was quite a thrilling thing to watch for their hatching. The Doctor usually gave each specimen at least a day's freedom in the little indoor flower garden, which was prepared for his reception, before experimenting on him with the listening apparatus.

But one of the early discoveries we made was that the

language, such as it was, had been apparently known to the insects before they were born into the flying state.

"I imagine, Stubbins," said the Doctor, when we were discussing this curious fact one day, "that one of the reasons for this is that the insects already have some life experience in the caterpillar form. Then the methods of conveying their ideas, which we call a language, cannot be called, after all, actual talking, in which the tongue has to be trained to make sounds. And for the rest, there is no doubt that this form of life inherits a lot more experience and training than we or the larger animals do. Their memories go farther back, beyond the short term of their own life, and carry over impressions and ideas that really belong to the herd—to the species."

This knowledge of things that lay outside their own experience in the moths and butterflies interested the Doctor a great deal. The case of the gentlemen visitors who mysteriously found their way to the Doctor's house to call on the lady hawk was not, by any means, the only example of the astonishing things these creatures could do.

When it came to trying to find out *how* they accomplished these mysterious feats we discovered we were against a hard problem. They themselves did not seem to know how they found their way about as soon as they were born, how they knew the way to the kind of leaves and food they wanted, etc.

They seemed to be born also with a quite unexplainable store of legends and history about their own species and a knowledge of the enemies that they must avoid if they wished to survive. All they could tell us when we came to question them on *how* they got this knowledge was that they *knew* it.

"You know, Stubbins," said the Doctor, "that is what is called intuitive knowledge, by the philosophers, knowledge you are born with. With humans it is pretty small. As babies we know enough to cry when we want a bottle and we know enough to suck the bottle when it is given to us. That's about all. It isn't much. But it is something. Chickens, on the other hand, are born with a knowledge of how to walk and peck and how to run to their mothers when she gives the call of alarm if danger is near. That's better than we can do. But these fellows! Their intuitive knowledge is tremendous. Their mothers are nowhere near them when they come into the world. Yet they know how to fly, how to set about the whole business of life right away. But the part that fascinates me is their knowledge of legends and history belonging to their own breed. That's something quite new, as far as I know—and also the main thing that makes me so hopeful that we can learn a great deal of real scientific value from them. It is the intuitive knowledge which we humans are so short on."

He paused a moment, thoughtful and silent.

"You see, certain people," he presently went on, "are much better. You remember Long Arrow?"

"Yes, indeed," I said. "Could I—could anyone—forget him?"

"Nearly all," said the Doctor, "of that perfectly wonderful botany work that he did was accomplished by intuitive investigation. The same with his navigation and geography. I used to question him for hours, trying to find out how he had done these things. He didn't know. He just began along some line of instinct and followed it till he got results. Long Arrow! My gracious, what a wonder he was! The greatest scientist of them all. And the bigwigs up in

London, the Royal Society, The Natural History Museum, and the rest, they hardly know his name! When I tried to tell them about him they thought I was cracked, a sort of Münchhausen romancing about his voyages . . . ah, well!"

This recalling of Long Arrow and our days on Spidermonkey Island put us both in a serious reminiscent mood. Chee-Chee, who had shared those days and adventures, had come into the study a moment or two before and was listening intently. I saw an expression on his face that told me he had the same thought in mind as I had. I turned back to the Doctor, who had moved over to the window and was once more gazing up at the full moon, which flooded the garden outside with a ghostly light.

"Listen, Doctor," I said, "supposing you sought out Long Arrow again: isn't it quite possible, with his great knowledge of this intuitive kind of investigation, that he might be able to help you with your study of the moths—the language of insects? He has probably already done a great deal in the same direction himself."

I saw from the quick manner in which the Doctor swung away from the window and faced me that my dodge to get him again interested in the idea of voyages had had effect. But almost at once he frowned as though a second thought had interfered.

"Oh, but, Stubbins," said he, "goodness only knows where Long Arrow may be now. He never stayed many months, as you remember, in any place. It might take years to find him."

"Anyhow," said Chee-Chee, speaking up for the first time, "I don't see why you shouldn't go to Spidermonkey and take up the trail. You hadn't any more idea of his whereabouts last time you set out to seek him. And yet you found him."

Again the Doctor paused. I knew the wanderlust was on him—as it was on me, Chee-Chee, and Polynesia. Yet he evidently felt that in following his impulse he was running away from a serious and important work.

"But, Chee-Chee," he said, "last time I had something to go on. Miranda, the purple bird of paradise, had told me he was somewhere in the neighborhood of northern Brazil or Spidermonkey Island. While now? . . . No one on earth could tell us where to begin looking for him."

"Listen, Doctor," I said. "You remember the way we decided last time? You had given up all hope of finding him, when Miranda came and told you he had disappeared."

"Yes, I remember," said John Dolittle.

"So we played Blind Travel, the atlas game, you remember that?"

"Yes, I do," said the Doctor.

Chee-Chee shuffled along the floor and drew a little nearer.

"Well," said I, "why not play it again? You don't know where he is. Last time we had good luck. Maybe we'll have as good—or better—this time. What do you say?"

For some moments John Dolittle hesitated. He went back to the window, drew aside the curtains, and again gazed up at the moon.

"How beautiful she looks!" he muttered.

"Well?" I repeated. "What do you say? Shall we play Blind Travel?"

This appeal to the boy in him was evidently too strong.

The frown disappeared from his face and suddenly he smiled.

"I think it might be quite a good idea, Stubbins. It is suppertime, I fancy. Bring along the atlas and I'll meet you in the kitchen."

· The Fourteenth Chapter ·

BLIND TRAVEL AGAIN

CHEE-CHEE was overjoyed. As the Doctor left the study to go to the kitchen, I moved toward the bookcase. But the agile monkey was there before me. Scaling up the shelves as though they were a ladder, he had the big volume down off the top in less time than it takes to tell it. Together we carried it to the table and laid it down.

"Oh, my, Tommy," he whispered, "we're in luck!"

He began opening the pages. The first—how well I remembered it!—title page: *"ATLAS OF THE WORLD. Giving the Latest Discoveries in Africa, the Arctic, and Antarctic Continents, etc. Published by Green and Sons, Edinburgh, in the year,"* etc., etc. Then came the astronomic page—the signs of the zodiac; phases of the moon; precession of the equinoxes, etc., etc.

"The moon!" muttered Chee-Chee. "Poor old Doctor! He seems to have gone almost balmy about the moon. My, but look at all the lands we might visit! Come on, Tommy, let's get to the kitchen and make him begin before he changes his mind."

Grabbing a sharp pencil off the Doctor's desk, I took the heavy volume under my arm and followed Chee-Chee out of the room.

In the kitchen we found all the family seated about the table waiting for us: Bumpo, Gub-Gub, Too-Too, Jip, and the white mouse.

"Ah," said the Doctor, "you have the atlas, Stubbins—and a pencil? Good! Just hold back the dinner a moment, Dab-Dab, will you, while we see where we are to go?"

"Go? Go? What does he mean?" asked Gub-Gub of Chee-Chee in an excited whisper.

"He has consented to play Blind Travel with us," Chee-Chee whispered back.

"What on earth is that?" asked Gub-Gub.

"Oh, you open the atlas with your eyes shut and put a pencil down. And whatever point it hits, that's the place you've got to go. Goodness, I'm all of a flutter! I do hope it's somewhere in Asia. I want to see the East."

Well, if Chee-Chee was in a flutter, as he called it, Gub-Gub was even more agitated over this momentous game we were about to play. He kept running around to a different place at the table, jumping up on someone else's chair, being sat on, upsetting people, overturning furniture, and generally getting the whole gathering frazzled and confused.

Not that any of us were what you could call calm. A very great deal depended on this strange game that the Doctor had invented when he was a young man. Then it only affected him. In those days he was a free, unattached bachelor and this odd method of determining his destination meant very little difference so far as preparations were concerned. But now (I did not yet know how many of the household he meant to take with him) its outcome might mean much for several of us.

"Listen," said the Doctor when he had the big book laid in the center of the table: "Last time Stubbins held the pencil. How would it be if Bumpo did it this time? He is a lucky individual, I know."

"All right," said Bumpo. "But I hope I don't send you all to the middle of the Specific Ocean." (He was turning over the first few pages and had paused at one illustrating the proportions of the globe in land and water.)

"That's all right," said the Doctor. "One of the rules of the game is that if your pencil falls on water, you have a second try. And the same thing applies if you touch a town or a district where you have been before. You keep on trying till you strike land, land that you have never visited. Then you have to go there—have to—somehow."

"Very good," said Bumpo taking up the pencil and closing the book. "I hope this is one of my lucky nights."

"I hope so too," whispered Gub-Gub, nosing up his snout onto the table between the Doctor's elbow and mine. "I would like a warm country where there is plenty of sugarcane. It's years since I tasted sugarcane. In the Canaries, it was, when we were hiding away from those wretched pirates. You remember, Polynesia?"

· The Fifteenth Chapter ·
GUB-GUB HALTS THE GAME

IT WAS quite a picture, that group around the table—and it will never fade from my memory while life lasts. Bumpo was the only one standing. He held the pencil in his right fist. His left hand grasped the atlas, closed, and resting on the back of its binding, ready to let it fall open at whatever page Fate should decide. The rest of us were seated around in a circle tense with excitement, watching him. Four candles burned on the table in brass sticks. For a moment you could have heard a pin drop, so perfect was the silence.

"Are you quite ready, Bumpo?" asked the Doctor in a strangely steady voice. "Remember, you close your eyes, let the book fall open, and then stab down with the pencil point."

"Yes, Doctor," said Bumpo. "I'm quite ready."

"Splendid!" said the Doctor. "Go ahead."

Bumpo let go his left hand. The heavy book fell open with a *bang.* His right fist, describing circles in the air with the pencil, slowly lowered the point . . . Then—*crash!*

Gub-Gub in his eagerness to learn where we were to go had rocked the table as he lurched forward, and all four candles toppled over. The room was in darkness.

At once a babel of voices broke out everywhere. Everyone shouted advice at once. But the Doctor's was too emphatic to be drowned.

"Hold it, Bumpo!" he cried. "Don't move your pencil. We will have a light here in a moment. Keep your pencil where it is."

Of course, as is always the way, the matches were *not* handy. Dab-Dab, whacking poor Gub-Gub over the ears with her wing, started out to find them. She was quite a long time about it. But soon we began to see dimly, anyhow. For the full moon that flooded the garden outside the windows made it possible to make out the general shape of everything in the room. One of the curtains had not been completely drawn across.

"It's all right, Doctor," said Bumpo. "I'm hanging on to it. Get a match and let's see where we are to go."

The excitement, as you can imagine, was tremendous. The moonlight in the room was enough to see one another by but not enough to read by.

"I'll bet it's Africa," said Polynesia. "Well, I don't know as I shall mind—much. It *is* a good country."

"It isn't Africa," said Too-Too. "I know it."

"What is it then?" we all cried, remembering that Too-Too could see in the dark.

"I shan't tell," said Too-Too. "But you can take my word for it. It's a surprise! Yes, it's certainly a surprise. We shall need all the money we can raise for *this* voyage."

"Oh, do please hurry up with the matches, Dab-Dab!"

"Tripped over a mat and fell into a pail"

cried Gub-Gub. "I shall burst if I don't know soon where we're going. And this moonlight is giving me the jimjams."

So intent was he on getting a light he left the table and groped his way out of the door to assist the housekeeper in her search. All he succeeded in doing, however, was to bump into her in the dark as she came in with her wings full of a fresh supply of candles and the much-needed matches. Completely bowled over by her collision with the portly Gub-Gub, Dab-Dab dropped the matches, and in the scuffle they were kicked away into some corner where they couldn't be found.

Among us who remained in the kitchen the general excitement was not lessened by the sounds of Gub-Gub getting spanked and pecked by the indignant duck. Squeaking, he ran for the scullery, where from further noises that followed, he apparently tripped over a mat and fell into a pail.

At last the Doctor himself went to the rescue. He succeeded in reaching the larder without mishap, where he found another box of matches and came back to us with a light shaded in his hands.

As the first beam fell across the open atlas my heart gave a big thump. Bumpo rolled his eyes toward the ceiling. Polynesia gave a loud squawk. While Chee-Chee hissed beneath his breath a long low hiss of consternation.

The book had fallen open at the astronomic page. Bumpo's pencil had landed in a smaller illustration down in the left-hand corner. And its point still rested right in the center of the moon!

PART THREE

· The First Chapter ·

BUMPO AND MAGIC

THE Doctor himself was, I think, the only one who made no remark at all. Silent and thoughtful, he stood gazing down at the atlas over which Bumpo's fist still hung, holding the pencil point into the heart of the moon.

"Shiver my timbers!" growled Polynesia, hitching herself along the table with her funniest sailor gait. "What a voyage, my lads, what a voyage! Yes, it's the moon all right. Well, I suppose he might have hit the sun. Its picture's there and all the other blessed heavenly bodies. Could be worse."

"I wonder," said Gub-Gub, who had returned from the scullery and was now also leaning over the page, "what sort of vegetables they have in the moon."

"Tee-hee!" tittered the white mouse. "Such a joke I never heard!"

"I don't see why there shouldn't be rats," said Jip. "The moon always looks to me as though it was full of holes."

"It should be a cheap place to live," said Too-Too. "I don't suppose they use money there at all."

" 'Shiver my timbers!' growled Polynesia"

"Yes, but it would cost a pretty penny to get there, don't forget!" muttered Dab-Dab.

"All right," said the housekeeper finally breaking up the discussion with a more practical voice, "supper is getting cold. If you'll take that wretched book off the table, Tommy, we will bring in the soup."

"But shouldn't we play it over again, Doctor?" asked Jip. "That's a place no one could get to, the moon. We are entitled to another try, are we not? according to the rules of Blind Travel."

"Maybe," snapped Dab-Dab, "according to the rules of Blind Travel, but not according to the rules of this kitchen —not before supper, anyway. The food's been delayed half an hour, as it is. Sit down, everyone, and let's begin before it is ruined entirely."

We all took our places at the board and the meal was begun in rather an odd general silence, which was broken only by Gub-Gub's noisy manner of drinking soup.

"Well, anyway, Doctor," said Bumpo after a few moments, "you couldn't get there, could you? To the moon, I mean."

"Oh, I wouldn't go so far as to say that, Bumpo," replied the Doctor. "On the contrary, I'm convinced someone will some day get there. But of course for the present until science has provided us with new methods of aerial travel it is pretty much out of the question. As a matter of fact, in a way, I'm glad the game turned out in the fashion it did. I was already beginning to regret that I had promised Stubbins and Chee-Chee we would play it. I really should stick to my work here. I am awfully keen to get to the bottom of this story the moths told me about a giant race. The more I think of that, and the further I follow it up, the surer I become that it has a foundation of truth."

"You mean you won't take another try at Blind Travel, Doctor?" said Chee-Chee in a sadly disappointed voice.

"Well," said John Dolittle, "I have fulfilled my promise, haven't I? The pencil struck land that no one could reach, for the present, anyhow. If you'll show me some way I can get to the moon, we'll go. In the meantime—well, we have our work to do."

· The Second Chapter ·

THE TAPPING ON THE WINDOW

AND so there followed the general feeling of acute disappointment. The whole household, with the possible exception of Dab-Dab (and I'm by no means sure she, too, would not have welcomed the idea of a voyage at this time), had been keyed up to the promise of departure for foreign shores. Now with the prospect of remaining home indefinitely, there was quite a letdown all around. Promptly, remarks began to break forth.

"Well, but, Doctor," said Chee-Chee, "how about Long Arrow? You agreed that he might be most helpful in this study of insect language and er—what did you call it?—intuitive investigation. Are you going to give up the idea of consulting him, just because Bumpo struck the astronomic page in the atlas?"

"Chee-Chee," said the Doctor, "didn't I tell you that I don't know where he is and that I know of no way of finding out? I agree he might be most helpful—and perhaps the only scientist in the world who could aid me. But if I don't know where he is, how can I get at him?"

This argument convinced me and, I must confess, saddened me quite a little. For I had really set my heart on a voyage with John Dolittle, which was an experience, I knew, like nothing else in life. But to my great joy another ally came to the aid of Chee-Chee and myself.

"Doctor," said Polynesia suddenly and severely, "you know you are just trying to fool us. Do you mean to say that with *your* knowledge of the animal world you couldn't find out where that man is—with all the birds and the beasts and the fishes of the seven seas more than anxious to assist you in anything you want? Tut-tut!"

The Doctor, for a moment, looked almost guilty. And I suddenly realized that he had taken advantage of the outcome of our game of Blind Travel to put off any voyage for the present, deliberately, because he felt he ought to stick to his work at home.

"Oh, well, Polynesia," he said finally in some little confusion, "you must admit I have fulfilled my promise. We have obeyed the rules of the game. The land we hit on was an impossible destination. I repeat: if you can show me a way to get to the moon, I'll take you there."

The shrewd old parrot, who had, after all, given John Dolittle his first lessons in animal language, was not easily fooled. She put her head on one side, dropped the piece of toast she had been chewing, and regarded him with a very knowing expression.

"You haven't answered my question, Doctor," said she. "Do you, or do you not, believe it is impossible for you to find out where Long Arrow now is?"

"Well," said John Dolittle, "you remember what a dickens of a job we had in finding him last time we set out to hunt him?"

"Yes," said Polynesia, "but that was because he had gotten trapped in the cave by the falling rocks. If he is free now, as he probably is, it would be no great matter—for you."

For a moment the Doctor squirmed in his chair. Polynesia was the best arguer I have ever known.

"But don't you see," he said at last, spreading out his hands in front of him, "I have such a tremendous lot of work here still unfinished. I told you this legend the moths spoke of, about a race of giants—moths as big as a house, who could lift a ton weight as though it were an ounce. That is something that must be looked into. Goodness only knows what it might lead to."

"And goodness only knows what your going abroad might lead to, either," said Polynesia. "But the truth is, I suppose, you just don't want to go. You're tired of just ordinary exploration and voyaging. The moon is the only thing that would satisfy you—like a baby."

A little silence fell on the assembly. Dab-Dab had not yet begun to clear away. Everybody seemed to be thinking hard.

And then there came the most mysterious tapping on the window, an odd, heavy, muffled sort of tapping.

"Boo!" grunted Gub-Gub, "Spookish!" and he crawled under the table.

"I'm not going to pull back the curtains," said Bumpo, "—not for a fortune. You go, Tommy."

I was after all the nearest to that window. I guessed it was Cheapside, as usual, asking to come in. But I should have known. No sparrow ever made a noise like that. I swung aside the curtains and gazed out into the moonlit garden. Then I clapped my hand to my mouth to stop the yell of surprise that rose to my lips.

· The Third Chapter ·

THE GIANT RACE

I SHALL never forget the feeling I had as my eyes made out the strange picture there on the lawn beneath the eerie light of the moon. It wasn't so much that I was frightened but that I was astonished, overwhelmed—so overwhelmed that for some moments after I had stifled my first impulse to yell, I could not speak at all. Presently I looked back at the Doctor and opened my mouth but no words came.

"What is it, Stubbins?" said he rising and joining me at the window.

Used as John Dolittle was to strange sights and unusual things, this vision outside the glass for a moment staggered even him. There was a face looking in at us. To begin with it took one quite a while to realize that it *was* a face. It was so large that you did not take it in or see the connection, at first, among the various features. In fact the entire window, at least six feet high by three feet wide, only encompassed part of it. But there was no mistaking the eyes—strange and very beautiful eyes. Anyone but those who, like the Doctor and myself, were intimately familiar with the anatomy of insects, would quite possibly have taken them for something else. But to us, in spite of their positively gigantic size, they were unmistakably the eyes of a moth.

Set close together, bulging outward, shimmering like vast iridescent opals in the pale candlelight from the room, they made us feel as though we were gazing through a powerful magnifying glass at an ordinary moth's head.

"Heaven preserve us!" I heard the Doctor mutter at my elbow. "It must be the giant race. Snuff the candles out, Stubbins. Then we'll be able to see the rest of him better."

With trembling hands I did as I was told—then sped back to the window and the fascination of this astonishing apparition. And now, when the candlelight did not interfere with the moon's rays in the garden, it was possible to see more. The moth positively seemed to fill the whole garden.

His shoulders behind the head, which was pressed close against the panes, towered up to a height of at least two storeys. The enormous wings were folded close to the thick, furry body, giving the appearance of the gable-end of a house—and quite as large. The enormous foot that had softly struck the window still rested on the sill. The great creature was quite motionless. And even before the Doctor spoke of it, I got the impression that he was injured in some way.

Of course the excitement among those in the room was terrific. Everyone, with the exception of Gub-Gub, rushed to the window and a general clatter broke forth that the Doctor at once hushed. Gub-Gub preferred the safety of his retreat beneath the table to any moonlight encounters with the supernatural.

"Come, Stubbins," said the Doctor, "get some lanterns and we will go out. Chee-Chee, bring me my little black bag, will you, please?"

Followed by Jip, Polynesia, and Too-Too, the Doctor hurried out into the back garden. You may be sure I was not far behind them with the lanterns—nor was Chee-Chee with the bag.

That whole night was one long procession of surprises. As soon as I got out into the garden I became conscious of something funny happening to my breathing. The air seemed unusual. As I paused, sniffing and half gasping, Chee-Chee overtook me. He, too, seemed to be affected.

"What is it, Tommy?" he asked. "Feels like sniffing a smelling bottle—sort of takes your breath away."

I could give him no explanation. But on reaching the Doctor we found that he also was suffering from some inconvenience in breathing.

"Give me one of those lanterns, Stubbins," said he. "If this moth is injured I want to see what I can do to help him."

It was a curious, fantastic sight. The Doctor's figure looked so absurdly small beside the gigantic form of his "patient." Also it was very hard to see at such close quarters and by such a small light where the patient left off and where the garden began. One enormous thing, which I had at first thought to be a tree he had knocked down in landing, turned out to be his middle left leg. It was hairy and the hairs on it were as thick as twigs.

"What do you reckon is the matter with him, Doctor?" I asked.

"I can't just tell yet," said John Dolittle, bending and peering around with his lantern. "His legs seem to be all right and I should judge that his wings are, too. Of course I couldn't get up to examine them without a good big ladder. But their position seems natural enough. It would almost appear as though exhaustion were the trouble. From the general collapsed condition of the whole moth he looks to me as though he were just dead beat from a long journey."

"What is this business that keeps catching our throats, Doctor?" asked Chee-Chee.

"The air is surcharged with oxygen," said the Doctor. "Though what the source of it is I haven't yet discovered. Possibly the creature's fur, or maybe his wing powder. It is quite harmless, I think, if a bit heady and exhilarating. Bring along that second lantern, Stubbins, and let's take another look at his head. How on earth he managed to land down on a lawn this size without ripping himself on the trees, I have no idea. He must be a very skillful flier in spite of his great size."

With the aid of the two lights we carefully made our way forward towards the creature's head, which was almost touching the side of the house. We had to pull bushes and shrubs aside to get up close.

Here we found the peculiar quality of the air, on which we had already remarked, more pronounced than ever. It was so strong that it occasionally made the head reel with momentary fits of dizziness but was not otherwise unpleasant. Lying on the ground beneath the moth's nose were several enormous orange-colored flowers. And the Doctor finally detected the oxygen, as he called it, as coming from these. We were both nearly bowled over as we stooped to examine them. The Doctor, bidding me also retire for a

" 'I don't think it's pure oxygen,' said the Doctor"

while, withdrew into the house, where from the surgery he produced cloths soaked in some chemical liquid to counteract the effect of the potent perfumed gas from the flowers. With these tied about our noses and mouths we returned to our investigations.

"I don't think it's pure oxygen," said the Doctor as he examined one of the enormous blossoms. "If it were, I don't imagine we could stand it even as well as this. It is a powerful natural scent given out by the flowers, which is heavily charged with oxygen. Did you ever see such gigantic blooms? Five of them. He must have brought them with him. But from where? And why?"

Bending down, the Doctor placed one of the flowers under the moth's nose.

"He couldn't have brought them for nothing," said he. "Let's see what effect their perfume has on him."

· The Fourth Chapter ·

THE AWAKENING OF THE GIANT

AT FIRST it appeared as though the Doctor's experiment was going to have no result. The huge head of the moth rested on the ground almost as if dead. But knowing how long even our own kinds of moths could stay motionless, we did not yet have any fears on that score.

"It's the position that's curious," muttered the Doctor, still holding the huge bell of the flower over the moth's nose. "The head is thrust forward in quite an unnatural pose. That's what makes me feel he may have actually lost consciousness from exhaustion . . . Oh, but see, wasn't that a tremor in the antennae?"

I looked up at the feathery palmlike wands that reared upward from the head (they reminded you of some fantastic decorations in the turban of a rajah), and, yes—there was no doubt of it—the ends were trembling slightly.

"He's coming to, Doctor," I whispered. "Hadn't you better stand farther away, in case he struggles to get up? To be stepped on by one of his feet would be no joke."

The Doctor's utter fearlessness in the presence of this unbelievable monster was quite typical. The animal king-

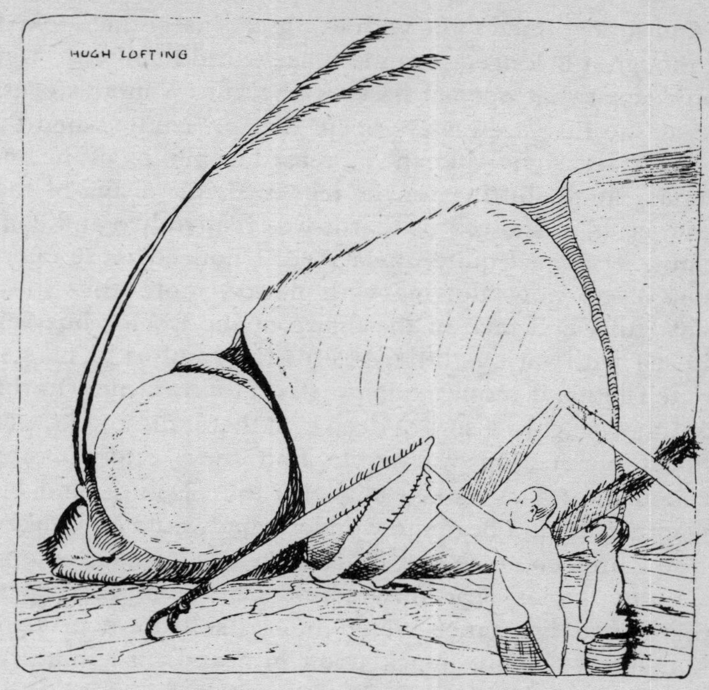

" 'Wasn't that a tremor in the antennae?' "

dom had no terrors for him. And a moth the size of a large building disturbed him no more, so far as his personal safety was concerned, than a new-born lamb. And that strange trust was always shared by the animals themselves. I have never seen any creature that was afraid of the Doctor or disposed to fight him. It was this perhaps, above all things, that set him apart among mankind and made him the naturalist he was. Every living thing appeared to have confidence in him from the moment it set eyes on him.

And so it seemed to be with this great insect that looked as though it belonged to some other world than ours. You could not say it opened its eyes—because a moth's eyes, having no lids, are always open. But, presently, when by various little signs—like the increased trembling of the antennae, small shiftings of the legs, a slight raising of the head, etc. —it showed us that it was really alive and conscious, it seemed quite unalarmed. I noticed those enormous eyes—now glowing with newer, more conscious, light—turn and take in the figure of the Doctor busying himself with various little jobs for the comfort of his patient. The giant moth made no struggle to get up. On the contrary, he gave a sort of deep sigh that indicated he was almost pleased on waking to find the Doctor fussing around him. As I looked at them, John Dolittle and his gigantic patient, I began to wonder what would have taken place if this creature had fallen into another garden and into other hands. Fear, on account of his great size, superstition, and ignorance would most likely have brought about some violent attack upon him and his unnatural death. I thought of Chee-Chee's prehistoric artist, Otho Bludge. Would not his first impulse have been to destroy this enormous creature as soon as it appeared—to be the first in attack, lest it destroy him?

But with the Doctor, no. Size, foreign characteristics, and qualities did not incur fear or distrust. On the contrary, anything new attracted him, always, rather than scared him. And by being with him I, in a lesser measure, had grown to share something of this confidence—even if I had not yet learned to impress the same feeling of trust on creatures I met with.

I was sharply reminded of what the Doctor had said

about intuitive knowledge also, as I watched these two. The moth, of course, could not speak one word of the Doctor's language nor the Doctor, so far, a syllable of the moth's. And yet, without language, they seemed to be conveying certain things to one another with fair ease. For example, the Doctor evidently wished to climb up and examine the moth's wing muscles, which he expected had been overstrained in the long flight. Somehow, goodness only knows by what means, he conveyed this idea to the patient. Anyway, it suddenly contracted its chest and let its front pair of legs spread apart, so that the summit of its shoulders was lowered a good ten feet. Then very carefully, lest he hurt the moth's skin, the Doctor clambered up in the deep fur that covered the middle trunk (I think he called it the *thorax*) until he stood where the enormous wings were joined to the body.

Up there where no rays from the lamp could reach him he was quite invisible to Chee-Chee and me. But presently he called down to me to open his little black bag and throw him up a bottle of liniment.

· The Fifth Chapter ·

KEEPING A SECRET

OF COURSE on an exciting occasion of this kind the Doctor, who always seemed to be able to do without sleep if necessary, outstayed all of us in the garden. Polynesia was deeply interested also, but by three o'clock in the morning she retired to the house and took a nap on top of the grandfather clock on the stair landing. Chee-Chee finally fell asleep under the bushes. I, by pinching myself at five-minute intervals, managed to carry on till dawn showed over the roof ridge of the house. Too-too, of course, could always apparently stay awake with more comfort during night hours than in daylight. He and the Doctor were, I think, the last left on deck. He told me next day that John Dolittle had not gone to bed before six A.M.

Staggering around the garden with one eye open and the other shut, I had managed to act the part of the Doctor's assistant almost as long as that. When I woke up (about two o'clock the following afternoon) I found myself on the hall settee with the carpet drawn over me for bedclothes. I learned, when I went to the kitchen and found Dab-Dab frying eggs, that John Dolittle had made the giant moth comfortable in the garden and was planning to see him early the following day.

Luckily the night had been mild. I took the cup of tea and piece of toast which Dab-Dab offered me and went out into the garden. Here, of course, I discovered the Doctor, who after a couple of hours' nap somewhere between six and nine in the morning, was continuing his study of the strange visitor. He had evidently been trying out various foods because great quantities of different edibles lay about the lawn. What strange instinct had guided the Doctor finally to honey I do not know, for certainly this giant specimen did not look like any of the honey-sucking moths with which we were familiar. But certainly John Dolittle had hit upon a food agreeable to the creature, even if it was not his natural one. When I came up to them he was just setting to on a new comb, while the empty frames of six others lay around him on the grass.

The Doctor had managed by this to get the moth to move back somewhat from the house. He now stood, or sat, comfortably, on the lawn; and while he occupied most of the turf, we could approach him from all sides and get a much better idea of what he looked like.

In color he was a light brown in the body with very gorgeous wings of red and blue. His legs were green, the rest of him black. In shape he was of the type that keeps the wings closely folded to the body when at rest, though, to be sure, his general lines and appearance were only vaguely suggestive of any species we knew among earthly moths.

"I moved him over here," said the Doctor, "so that there should be less chance of anyone seeing him from the front garden."

"I took the cup of tea and piece of toast that Dab-Dab offered me"

"But how did you manage to make him understand you wished him to move?" I said. "Can you speak his language already?"

"Oh, no—not a word," he said. "But . . . well . . . I suppose I really don't know just how I did it. I moved over there and beckoned to him and put the food down. And . . . well . . . anyhow, he seemed most well disposed toward me and anxious to cooperate in any way."

I laughed. "That, Doctor," I said, "is the thing that has

made you succeed in animal languages where so many naturalists have failed. I'm not so sure that Long Arrow was much better than you when it comes to doing things by instinct rather than by science. But why are you so afraid the people will see the moth?"

"Why, Stubbins," said he, "most important. If the townsfolk get wind of this extraordinary creature being here, we would be besieged, just besieged, by visitors. He doesn't like strangers. Of that I'm sure—naturally timid, you know, in spite of his size. No, whatever happens, his presence here must be kept secret. And by the way, if Matthew should call—and you know he usually drops in almost every night after supper—don't let him come into the back garden, whatever you do. We will have to bind Bumpo and the animals to secrecy in this. Because while Gub-Gub and Jip can't talk with Matthew, they might easily give the moth's presence away. And the one thing Matthew can't do is to keep a secret."

And so that afternoon we called the household together and swore them all to absolute secrecy. More than that, the Doctor was so afraid that someone might discover the moth's presence and spread the news abroad, he instituted a system of sentries. Bumpo, Jip, and I took it in turns to mount guard at the front gate to make sure than no one strayed in by accident. We did duty in three-hour shifts, night and day. To make extra sure, Too-Too and Polynesia, who were both good hands at keeping awake, watched alternately from the ridge of the roof, where they could see anyone approach from any direction.

And it was a good thing that we did take those precautions. I had never realized before how many people ordinarily came to our quiet establishment in the course of a

"Too-Too and Polynesia watched from the ridge of the roof"

day. Tradesmen's boys delivering groceries, animal patients calling at the surgery, people dropping in to ask the way, the man from the water company to look at the meter, peddlers who wished to sell things, etc., etc.

But with our system of sentries no one ever got a glimpse of the giant moth or a suspicion that he was hidden in the Doctor's garden.

"Have you any idea, Doctor," I asked one evening, "where this creature has come from?"

"As yet I have not," said he. "I have been trying to find

that out, as you can easily imagine, ever since he arrived. I have examined his feet most carefully, hoping that that might give me a clue. But so far it has led to nothing. I even put some particles of dust I found under a microscope. But I am sure, from my examination, that they were picked up after his arrival here in the garden—while landing, no doubt. What I hope to do now is to get into communication with him through some form of vibration record, just as we did with the ordinary moths and flies. But, of course, it isn't going to be easy with a creature of this size. We will have to devise special apparatus to fit the job. I fear it may take a lot of work. But it doesn't matter. I feel I am on the eve of discovering big things. I am quite content to spend a long time on this. It is worth it."

· The Sixth Chapter ·

THE BUTTERFLIES' PARADISE

AND thus we settled down, with our sentries to keep the world out, to try and get in touch with this strange creature who had visited us from parts unknown.

To begin with, of course, the Doctor, with his extraordinary knowledge of the moths and butterflies of almost every part of the civilized world, was able to eliminate a great deal of territory as an impossible source for the moth to have come from. He had one theory that he followed for quite a time, and that was that it had come from what is called the subarctic regions. Very little was known so far, he told me, about insect life in those parts.

Then he got another idea, very far removed from the first. He had noticed that the giant moth was very cold at night. John Dolittle was quite upset over this. He made all sorts of arrangements about warming the garden. He worried Dab-Dab to death by buying oil stoves by the dozen to set around the garden and supplemented these by hot-water bottles actually in hundreds. We had the most terrible time getting them in secretly because, of course, the dealers insisted on delivering them by wagon. But we had to be just as insistent and bring them up to the house ourselves. They of course wanted to know what on earth we were going to do with so many hot-water bottles. A small town is a difficult place to keep a secret in.

Then the Doctor, following up the idea that the moth might have come from the tropics, started to question Chee-Chee. He asked him if he had ever heard his grandmother speak of giant insects at any time.

Poor Chee-Chee thought very hard for quite a while. He could not seem to remember any occasion on which his grandmother had referred to such creatures. But presently he said, "Oh, wait now—yes, I remember, there *was* something."

"Good!" said the Doctor. "What was it?"

And all the animals, hoping for another of Chee-Chee's stories of the ancient world, gathered about him to listen with attention.

"Well," said he, "there is no record that I know of, of any such insects belonging to the tropics—I mean, especially to those parts—either in past times or nowadays. But I do remember my grandmother saying that in those days before there was a moon the world had no end of perfectly enormous creatures running about it and that Man had a terribly hard time to survive. This was particularly so at certain times when various species like the dinosaurs and some of the more dangerous animals multiplied in such quantities that they crowded everything else out of certain sections. It wasn't only by chasing Man and destroying him that they had made life hard for him. But, for instance, when a swarm of these giant lizards descended on a farm where he had been growing corn and raising a few

"A swarm of giant lizards descended"

goats, they would eat up the whole crop, roots and all, in a few minutes, or clear off all the natural turf down to the bare ground, so that there was nothing left for the goats to feed on."

"Yes, yes," said the Doctor, "but the insects, Chee-Chee. Do you recall your grandmother speaking of any giant moths, beetles, or butterflies?"

"Yes, I was coming to that," said the monkey. "She used to tell us of one time—again, in the days before there was a moon—when a certain valley lay for a considerable time undisturbed by most creatures. You see, although there was occasional crowding in some areas, the world at that time had lots and lots of room in it. And, as I was saying, in this quiet, forgotten valley a giant race of butterflies is said to have flourished. Of course, my grandmother never saw them. They were millions of years before her time, and she only handed on the story to us as she had heard it. But she said it was still believed that these butterflies with their wings outspread were a hundred paces across from tip to tip."

"Had your grandmother ever spoken of other giant insects, Chee-Chee," asked the Doctor, "—of moths, for example?"

"Oh, well," said the monkey, "when I called them butterflies I was merely thinking of the general term in our language for all big flies of that sort. It is quite possible that the insects she spoke of were really moths. In fact, I think it is more likely, since they appear to have been exceedingly strong; and moths would be stronger than butterflies, wouldn't they?"

"Er—yes—generally speaking," said the Doctor, "they would. But how do you know they were strong?"

"Well, it seems," said Chee-Chee, "that when Man first came into the valley he found it full of extraordinary flowers and vegetation of all kinds. The soil seems to have been very, very rich there. It had been a lake up in the hills many years before, simply filled with fish. Then, suddenly, through an earthquake or something, all the water drained away through a crack in the mountains and the fish, of course, died in the mud that was left. The smell of the rotting fish at first drove every living thing away. But it also seems to have fertilized the valley in a very extraordinary manner. After a while, of course, seeds from the ordinary wild flowers and weeds began blowing in across the mountains. They took root, sprouted, bloomed and died down. Then *their* seed was blown about and did the same thing. But the new seed was very much better than the old, for the plants from which it came had grown strong in the most fertile ground in the world. And so it went on, each spring bringing forth finer and larger plants until, they say, many little wild flowers that in other parts were no bigger than a button had become here gigantic blossoms growing on bushes as high as an elm tree.

"And, of course, where there are flowers, butterflies and moths and bees and beetles will always come. And thus in time this deserted valley, once a dried-up sea of mud, stinking of rotten fish, grew into a butterflies' paradise. It was set deep down in a canyon whose walls were sheer and unscalable. Neither man nor beast came to disturb this flower-filled playground where the butterflies and bees led a happy, gorgeous life of sunshine, color, and peace."

Chee-Chee's story of the butterflies' paradise—as did most of his yarns of the ancient world—got us all deeply interested. From Gub-Gub to the Doctor, we were all listening intently as the little monkey, squatting tailor-fashion on the corner of the table, retold the legends of prehistoric times, which his ancestors had handed down to him.

"Well," he went on, "as it was with the flowers that fed and grew larger on the rich soil of the valley, so it was with the butterflies and bees who fed on the flowers. They became enormous. The honey they got from the blossoms made—"

"Excuse me," the Doctor interrupted. "Honey, did you say?"

"A party of baboons was the first to enter it"

"Yes," said Chee-Chee, "that was the food they got from the flowers, of course. So it was believed that it was the honey, peculiarly rich in that district, that made them so big."

"Humph! Yes, yes. Pardon me. Go on," said the Doctor.

"But naturally sooner or later such an extraordinary valley, filled with such extraordinary creatures, would have to be discovered and disturbed by strangers. There was a tradition among the monkey people, my grandmother said, that a party of baboons was the first to enter it. They, however, when they had finally scaled the rocky heights surrounding the canyon and looked down into the valley filled with gaudy-colored flies as big as ships, were so scared that they bolted and never went back there again. But some men who had watched the baboons climbing up, and made a note of how they reached the top, followed over the same trail. Among this party there was one very bold spirit who often led the others in attacks upon the large animals. While the others hung back in hesitation he descended the breakneck precipices, determined to investigate those lovely giants. He reached the bottom and there, from the ambush of an enormous leaf, big enough to hide a regiment under, he suddenly sprang out onto one of the butterflies as he crawled over the ground in the sun. The big insect, thoroughly frightened, took to his wings at once; and with the wretched man clinging to his shoulders, he soared away over the mountaintops. Neither of them was ever seen again."

· The Seventh Chapter ·

THE HOME OF THE GIANT MOTH

A GENERAL chatter of comment and criticism broke out around the kitchen table as Chee-Chee brought his story to an end.

"It's a good yarn, Chee-Chee," said Gub-Gub, "quite good. But I don't like it as well as the one about Otho Bludge."

"Why, Gub-Gub?" the Doctor asked.

"Oh, well," said the pig, "Otho's story was more romantic. I have a natural preference for romantic stories. I liked that part about the bracelet of stone beads that Pippiteepa left on the rock behind her—which Otho took and wore on his own wrist the rest of his days. That's a very romantic idea. It is dreadfully sad that he never met her anymore. I wish Chee-Chee would tell us that one over again."

"Some other night, perhaps," said the Doctor. "It is getting late now and we should be thinking of bed."

The Doctor was almost as interested in the great orange-colored flowers that the moth had brought with him as he was in the moth himself. To begin with, he had almost immediately on discovering them taken the greatest pains to preserve the great blooms. Huge quantities of ice (which was quite an expensive luxury in Puddleby) were procured from the fishmonger to keep the flowers fresh as long as possible. Meantime, John Dolittle experimented with one specimen to find out what gases its perfumes contained, etc.

The work apparently proved very interesting for him. He was quite good at analytical chemistry and he told me that the flowers presented problems that he felt had never been encountered by chemists before.

When he was done with this he turned his attention again to the moth himself but took precautions, in the meantime, that the remaining flowers should be given the best of care and made to last as long as possible.

In his study of the moth, progress was slow. If it had not been for the fact that the giant insect itself was most kindly disposed towards his investigations and did his best to help the Doctor in every way, I doubt if he would have gotten anywhere. But one day I gathered from the fact that John Dolittle had stayed out on that particular subject for nearly twenty-four hours at a stretch, and had missed his night's sleep altogether, that he was most likely achieving something important.

Well, the outcome of these long sessions of study on the Doctor's part was that one very early morning he rushed into my room, his eyes sparkling with excitement.

"Stubbins," he said, "it's too good to be true. I'm not certain of anything yet, but I think—I *think,* mind you—that I've discovered where this creature comes from."

"Goodness!" I said. "That's news worth a good deal. Where?"

"I guessed," he said, "that it couldn't be Europe. The

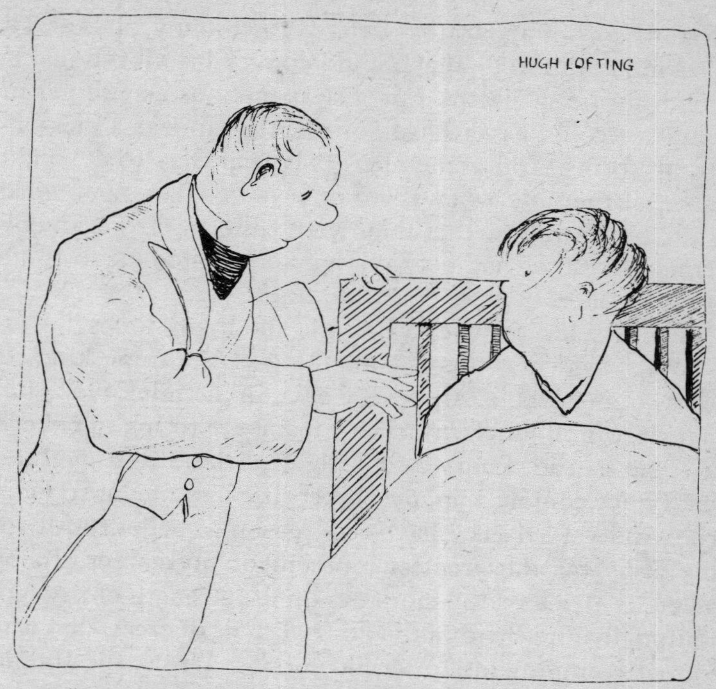

"One very early morning he rushed into my room

more remote corners of the world, like the subarctic and the tropics, didn't quite—well, they didn't exactly fit in, either."

"Anyway, you know now," I said. "Tell me quick; I'm dying to hear."

"I have every reason," he said, looking sort of embarrassed lest I should disbelieve him, "to suppose that *he comes from the moon!*"

"Heaven preserve us!" I gasped. *"The Moon?"*

"I have very little doubt," he answered. "I managed to rig

up some sort of apparatus—after a good many trials and a good many failures—that should convey his vibrations. If it had not been that he was just as anxious as I to get in contact, I could never have done it. He came as a messenger, it seems. You remember Polynesia has told you, I know, of the time when the monkeys in Africa sent word to me by a swallow that they were suffering from an epidemic—that they had heard of me and wanted me to come to the rescue?"

"Yes," I said, "Polynesia has told me many times."

"Well," said he, "this is something of the same kind. It seems unbelievable. And every once in a while I wake up, as it were, and pinch myself for fear I am trying to believe in some extraordinary and delightful dream—something that I have conjured up myself because I wanted it so to be true. And yet I think I have real reason to believe it. If so, this is by far the greatest moment of my career. To be called to Africa by the monkeys on the strength of my reputation, to cure them in the hour of their distress, that was a great compliment. To let loose Long Arrow, the Indian naturalist, from his prison in the cave, that was a moment well worth living for. But to be summoned to another world by creatures that human eyes have never seen before, that, Stubbins, is—"

He waved his hand without further words. His voice sounded strangely chokey. It was not often that I have seen John Dolittle overcome by emotion.

· The Eighth Chapter ·

FLOWERS OF MYSTERY

ANYONE can imagine what excitement this statement of the Doctor's would cause. All sorts of visions and possibilities passed before my mind. But so anxious was he that no false alarm should be spread abroad till he was certain of his facts, that he strictly forbade me to whisper a word of the matter to anyone. Nothing annoyed him so much as the half-baked announcements of scientists promising all sorts of wonders that never come true. And it must be said that he himself never published a word that he was not prepared to stand by and prove.

Before many days had passed, we decided that the flowers the moth had brought with him were almost as complicated a mystery as the great insect himself. The Doctor was, as I have said, in constant anxiety lest they should wither. It was not to be hoped, of course, that they would last more than a few days. His progress with the moth's language continued to be tantalizingly slow; and every morning he would go to the little special greenhouse where he kept the blossoms, expecting to find his treasures had wilted and passed away. But morning after morning they seemed as fresh as ever; and he was greatly puzzled. The ice and spraying and other care we gave them could not account for such extraordinary endurance.

The Doctor was pretty good at botany, as he was in all branches of natural history. He found on careful examination that the flowers had certain bulbous knobs just where the stem joined the bell of the blossom itself. These he told me were something quite different from the anatomy of any flower known to the earth's vegetable kingdom. Of course he had long since supposed that if the moth came from the moon, he brought the flowers also from that world. He was sure that these knobs, or glands, as he called them, accounted for the flower being able to endure so long in a state of perfect freshness after it had been plucked from its plant. He wondered if all moon flowers had the same quality.

But what mystified us a great deal more was that the flower apparently had the power to actually *move* itself—not only to change its position from that in which it had been laid down but also, we finally proved, to shift itself from place to place.

The way the Doctor discovered that peculiar quality of the moon bells, as we called the flowers, was this: he was in the habit of bringing one of the blossoms twice a day to the moth to smell. He had discovered that the insect derived great benefit from this daily tonic. He told me he was sure that the moon moth found our earthly atmosphere entirely too sluggish and lacking in oxygen. If we left him for more than about twelve hours without a sniff, he got sleepier and sleepier and would finally almost collapse.

At nighttime, after the moth had had his final sniff, the

Doctor always took the blooms back to the special ice-cooled conservatory to be stored till the next day. Of the five blooms, he used each one conscientiously in turn—thinking thus to economize the precious perfume. But that, by the way, proved to be unnecessary. For the flowers were as good a tonic at the end of the week as they were when we first discovered them. This treatment, with vast quantities of honey for food (which we actually supplied to the insect in barrowloads), was practically the only treatment that we gave our strange visitor.

Well, as I said, the Doctor would, with the greatest care, take the flowers back to the greenhouse and lay them down on a thick bed of asparagus fern. But the following morning, as regular as clockwork, he would find the flowers in different positions.

In the beginning, he had not laid any importance to this. But one evening he had put a bloom down almost touching the door of the conservatory because the others were occupying almost the entire space of the small house with their enormous bulk. When he came in the morning, expecting to find the flower he had used the night before close against the door, he was astonished to see that it and all the blossoms had rolled away toward the far end, and that last night's one had swung right around, so that the stem instead of the bell was facing the door.

At first he thought someone must have been in during the night and shifted the flowers. But the same thing occurred the following day. As usual he didn't speak of it to me till he was sure of his facts. We sat up one night and watched with a lantern, and both of us distinctly saw the flower nearest the door roll over and change its position.

At first, for my part, I wasn't satisfied.

"Why, Doctor," I said, "that could have been an accident. The way the flower was laid on the uneven bed of fern could account for its rolling a short distance like that!"

"All right," said he, "we will watch again tomorrow night. I am convinced—and I think I can prove to you—that the flowers do not like the draft from the door. They move away from it of their own accord, by rolling."

So the next night we repeated our watch. And this time I was completely convinced. We put two flowers close against the door. After about an hour one of them deliberately began to roll away toward the other end of the conservatory. A little later the other followed, both crowding in on the remainder of the specimens, huddling like sheep that wished to escape a storm. I could hardly believe my eyes. There was no question of accident here.

On our way back to the house the Doctor said, "You know, Stubbins, I feel we are here presented with an almost entirely new problem. There are flowers in our own vegetable kingdom that catch flies and close up at night and things like that. But one that can move itself after it is cut off from its plant is something quite new. You know, Stubbins—er—of course"—the Doctor hesitated a moment in one of his moods of half embarrassment, which had been pretty common of late—"er—this whole thing is so new and perplexing—but, well, I've had a notion for some days now that those flowers can communicate with one another."

"You mean that *they can talk!*" I cried.

"Just that," said he. "The way that they arrange themselves when they crowd up together at the far end of the conservatory—and—and I have even thought I could detect some exchange of conversation. But, of course, as I said, it is all so new. I may be wrong."

"Goodness!" I said. "That's a new idea, with a vengeance, isn't it?"

"It is," said he. "But in the moon? It may be the oldest idea there is—that flowers can talk. Certainly you and I have evidence already that they can think—and move."

· The Ninth Chapter ·

SMOKE ON THE MOON

THE night following that on which we had finally determined that the moon bells could move of their own accord I came into the Doctor's study about nine o'clock. At first I thought there was no one in the room and was about to go out to the kitchen. But presently I heard Polynesia whisper, "Is that you, Tommy?"

And then I made out Chee-Chee's form also squatting on the floor by the window.

I must confess that by this time I was getting sort of prepared for anything. I had even told my parents that I might leave any day on a voyage for parts unknown. The Doctor had become so—so secretive. Try as hard as I might to keep track of what was going on, I still had an uncomfortable feeling that John Dolittle was making discoveries and plans that he was telling to no one—at least not to me. That feeling had disturbed me a great deal.

"Yes, Polynesia," said I. "This is Tommy. What's going on here?"

"Oh," said she—and I knew at once from the tone of her

voice that she was on her guard—"the Doctor is just taking a few observations through his new telescope."

I realized right away that the Doctor was doing nothing of that kind. He *was* looking through his new telescope, it was true—an instrument that it had cost him just mints of money to buy. He had even kept its purchase a secret from Dab-Dab, who always scolded him whenever he laid out large sums on scientific instruments. But I saw at once that he wasn't taking observations.

"What are you doing, Doctor?" I asked, coming up to where he handled the telescope in the dark.

"Oh, well, Stubbins," said he, "I'm—er—I'm trying to see if they're signaling."

"What do you mean . . . they? . . . signaling?" I asked.

"Well, you see," said he, "I thought that if they sent down this moth with some sort of a message to me—which I really believe they did—that maybe they, those folks in the moon—I have no idea yet what sort of creatures they are, of course—would possibly give out some sort of signal to get in touch with him and see how his expedition was getting on . . . There! Did you see that? I'll swear I saw a puff—a sort of puff of smoke coming out from the moon's left side. You look in, Stubbins. Maybe I'm dreaming again!"

I looked into the telescope. But I must confess I could see little beyond the ordinary map of the moon. This I was already somewhat familiar with. The Doctor had several pamphlets issued by various astronomical observatories that gave details and maps of that side of the moon that was the only one we earthly people had ever seen. He and I had, during the last few days, studied these with a good deal of interest and attention. The Doctor himself was very familiar, I knew, with everything that had been learned

"He was looking through his new telescope"

and published on moon geography up to that time. He seemed disappointed when I told him I could see nothing unusual in the moon's appearance tonight.

"Strange—very strange!" he muttered. "I could have sworn I saw something—like a cloud, suddenly appearing and then fading away like smoke, on the left side. But there! This is all new. So much of it is guesswork as yet. And I'm always afraid that I'm being carried away by my own ideas and hopes."

I must confess that for my part I felt he had on this

occasion been misled, until I happened to meet Too-Too later in the evening, coming off duty from his post on top of the roof. He and Polynesia still took it in turns religiously to watch for intruders visiting the Doctor's premises who might hear of the moth's presence in his garden and carry the news abroad before the Doctor wished it known.

The little owl whispered that he would like to see me alone a minute. I took him onto my shoulder and proceeded upstairs to my room. There, with his usual accurate behavior in the complete darkness, he found the matches for me, carried them to the candle, and rattled them till I found my way to him.

"Shut the door, Tommy," said he mysteriously as soon as I had struck a light, "and take a look outside to make sure no one has followed us."

This I did.

"Well," said I, coming back to where he stood blinking beside the lighted candle, "what is it, Too-Too? Has anyone heard about the moth being here?"

"No," said he. "So far, I think I can say with absolute certainty the moth's presence here is a secret. Though I have serious fears about that gossip Gub-Gub. If he tells any other pigs, you can be sure we'll have all the porkers in the neighborhood nosing around to see what's going on. But as yet, I fancy, he hasn't had a chance. That's not the point. What I wanted to see you about was this: Did you happen to look at the moon at all this evening?"

"Yes," I said, "I looked at it through the Doctor's new telescope. Why?"

"Did you see anything—er—unusual?" he asked.

"No," I said, "I did not. The Doctor asked me the same

question. He was sure he had seen something out of the ordinary."

"Ah!" grunted Too-Too. "There you are. I thought so."

"Why, what happened?" I asked.

"Well, you know," said he, "we owls are pretty familiar with the moon. Her phases are, I suppose, more important to us than to almost any animal family. The light, you understand, for hunting and traveling by night is very important. Well, tonight happened to be the full moon—exactly full at ten o'clock. I was looking up at it thinking how bright it would be in the woods for hunting—too bright, in fact—when suddenly I saw a small cloud puff out from the left side—like smoke, it was. It didn't last more than a couple of seconds and then it was gone. But—well, I'm sure it was done deliberately."

"How do you mean?" said I. "By someone in the moon itself?"

"Well, of course," replied the owl. "I know it most likely sounds crazy to you. But after all, there's no use you and I pretending to one another that we haven't guessed where this moth comes from, is there? We don't have to let the world in on this secret. But—well, after all, we *know,* don't we? If he hasn't come from the moon, where else could he have come from? And what's he doing here, hanging around in very uncomfortable circumstances? He has come for some purpose, hasn't he?"

· The Tenth Chapter ·
TOO-TOO'S WARNING

THE difference between Too-Too and Polynesia in this matter was very noticeable. Polynesia had seemed as though she wanted to keep things from me. Too-Too was for taking me into his confidence. I had had an uncomfortable feeling that the old parrot was looking toward some occasion where—as I mentioned before—the Doctor also might wish me to be left in ignorance regarding his plans. How far John Dolittle himself was in agreement with her in this and how far she was acting on her own, I did not know. But it had caused me a good deal of anxiety.

To find that Too-Too was willing and anxious to be quite frank with me cheered me up considerably.

"You mean," said I, "that this moth is staying here in the hopes that he may take the Doctor back with him to the moon?"

"What else?" said Too-Too, spreading out his wings in a funny, argumentative gesture. "After all, you know the great man's reputation. There's nothing very surprising in that it should have reached the moon. No one can say yet

" 'What else?' said Too-Too"

what their civilization up there may have grown into. But naturalists like John Dolittle are not born every day—nor every century. They want him, I suppose, to solve some problem. And you may be sure that the Doctor will not be slow to answer their call for help. And what is more, he will certainly keep his going a secret till the last possible moment."

"Humph!" I muttered. "You think, then, that he might hop off any minute?"

"I don't know," said Too-Too. "There is no telling. They

certainly haven't let *me* in on any secrets. But I'm sure that giant moth came with some orders about bringing the Doctor back with him. How long it may take the Doctor to learn enough of the insect's language to know what they want, I cannot tell. But if you are interested I would advise you to keep a very close watch on John Dolittle's movements for the next few days. A word to the wise, you know."

I pondered a moment before answering.

"All right," I said at last. "Thank you, Too-Too, for warning me."

"It was not only on your own account," said the owl, "that I dropped this word of caution. If he goes, we animals would be much happier if he had some other human with him. Getting to the moon is—well—a risky business, to say the least, and it is my guess that he will avoid taking any more company than he can possibly help, on account of the risk."

It was only very shortly after that conversation with Too-Too that I made it my business to question the Doctor about his plans.

"So it is true," I said, "that you have hopes of getting to the moon with the help of this moth?"

"Well," said he, "it will depend of course, on how things pan out. But, yes, I think I can certainly say that I have hopes in that direction. As I told you, it seems pretty certain now that this moth was sent down especially to fetch me."

"It is a very thrilling idea," said I. "But to be quite honest, I don't see how you're going to manage it. They say there is no air there, don't they?"

The Doctor shrugged his shoulders.

"There is animal life there, anyway," said he. "These moths can manage very well. It is probably a different kind of air, that is all. I am faced with the problem of finding out what sort of atmosphere it is they have there. Once I've done that I shall be in a very much better position to say whether or not the earthly human can subsist in the moon. I am beginning to come to the conclusion that up there the vegetable kingdom is relatively much more active and important than the animal kingdom. Of course that's only guesswork, so far. But everything points to it. I believe that the atmosphere, whatever air they have, is created or influenced very largely by the vegetable kingdom. That is why the moth brought along with him those flowers whose perfumes seem so important to him."

"But," said I, "scientists have said there is no water there, haven't they? That if there were, there would be clouds?"

"Oh, well," said the Doctor, shrugging his shoulders, "how do they know—without having been there? Perhaps the moon water is of a different kind—one that does not volatilize and go off into clouds, the way it does with us. Perhaps the air, the heat, is of a different kind. Who shall say? The only way to know is to go there and see."

"That's all very well," I replied. "But in the job of finding out, you could, so far as I can tell, very easily give your life, without anyone thanking you."

The Doctor pondered seriously a moment.

"Yes," he said at last, "I admit it may sound sort of crazy to most people. But I have a confidence in animals. The lunar animal kingdom wants me up there for something. As yet, I haven't been able to find out exactly what it is. But so far, all my life, as you know, I have trusted the animal kingdom and I have never had that confidence imposed on. If the moon animals want me, I'll go. And I have no fear about their finding a way to get me there—and a way to get me back."

"Humph!" I said. "But even if there should be air—of a sort—on the moon itself, there is none in between, is there? My understanding of this situation is that when you get away from the earth a certain distance, you come to the end of the air envelope. How can anyone fly when there is no air for his wings to beat against?"

Once more John Dolittle shrugged his shoulders.

"The moth managed it," he said. "I imagine that so far as a medium for flying is concerned, the gravity of the earth being stronger than the gravity of the moon, he was pulled down here, without much effort on his own part, as soon as he got outside the moon's attraction. That would make it look as though it were easier to get here *from* the moon that from here *to* the moon. However, the most important thing would seem to carry enough atmosphere with you to support life on the voyage."

"Is it far," I asked, "to the moon?"

"Far enough," said he. "But, after all, only about one fourteen-hundredth part of the distance to the sun. As soon as I am convinced that they, that is the moon's animal kingdom, wants to have me come, then I'll go. I'm not afraid. They will take care of me. If they can get one of their people down to me, I should be able to get up to them. It is merely a question of knowing conditions and making provisions for perfectly natural, if new, conditions."

Of course, when the Doctor put it in that way there was, after all, very little to be said. That sublime confidence of his in the animal kingdom, whether it was of the moon or

" 'Is it far,' I asked, 'to the moon?' "

the earth, overcame all difficulties in a manner that left you almost gasping. If the moon creatures wanted him, he would go. That was the end of the matter.

For the rest, everything now depended on the development of conversation between himself and the giant moth. We had successfully kept the secret of its presence with us from the outside world—so far.

"You know, Stubbins," said he to me one evening when we were talking this over, "I am not even telling the animals, my own household, I mean, about any plans I may have for a possible journey to the moon. One cannot be too careful. If it ever leaked out that I was contemplating such a thing, we would have a reporter from every paper in the country clamoring at our gates for an interview within twenty-four hours. The world may call me a crank. But anything sensational like this can start an avalanche of publicity that nothing will stop. Polynesia is about the only one I have taken into my confidence. I suspect, of course, that Too-Too, Chee-Chee, and Jip have some idea of what is going on. But I haven't discussed the matter with them and I know I can trust them to keep their suspicions to themselves."

"Have you," I asked, "decided yet, if you do go, whom you would take with you? I presume you hadn't thought of going entirely alone?"

"Um—er—" the Doctor murmured, "that is a bit hard to settle yet. The—er—well, the risks, you know, Stubbins, are great. There is no sense in trying to hide that. It is something so entirely new. Sometimes I feel I should take no one with me at all—that I haven't the right to. If I go alone and I fail to get back, well, I'll have given my life in a cause worthwhile. As I said, for my own safety I haven't much fears. But I'm not so sure that the same protection would necessarily be given to the rest of my party. I have made no final decisions yet. Polynesia I would like to take —and Chee-Chee. I feel they both might be very useful; but for the rest, much as I would like to have them with me, I think they are better off where they are—at home."

And now, of course, the most important question for me was: Would I, Tommy Stubbins, be of the Doctor's party on the voyage to the moon? I was almost afraid to ask the question of him direct. Never have I been so divided in my feelings about anything. One minute I was just crazy to go. The next I realized what a mad, wild expedition it was and felt that the chances of anyone returning alive from such a voyage were too slight to be worth mentioning. Then followed the picture of how I would feel if I let him go alone and stayed behind myself. That finally decided me. Scared blue as I was of the whole scheme, I knew I just had to do my utmost to accompany him. I *couldn't* let him go without me. The following evening I broached the subject.

"Doctor," I said, "you are, of course, counting on taking me with you on this trip?" (I felt it best to begin by supposing that he was.) "You would find it hard to do without a secretary, wouldn't you? There is bound to be an enormous lot of note-taking to be done, eh?"

I watched his face keenly as he pondered a moment before answering.

"Well—er—Stubbins," he began at length, "you know how I feel about taking anyone with me—even those animal friends of mine, members of my household, who have no one to mourn over their loss if they should not come back. And—er—in your case, Stubbins, you must realize that it is—quite difficult. Please do not think that I don't appreciate the fact that you want to share the dangers of this entirely new enterprise with me. I admit I would be more than glad of your company. I expect to be faced with situations when the companionship of another human might be a tremendous comfort and help. But—well, you know, Stubbins, as well as I do, how your parents would feel if I took you with me on such a trip. To the moon! Compared with that our other voyages look like a twopenny coach ride to the outskirts of London. Then again, remember, Stubbins, I am flying in the face of all scientific authority. Whatever my own doubts may be, the fact remains that all astronomers, from Newton down, who have studied the moon emphatically declare that no life can exist there—that the moon is a dead world. I am gambling, like Columbus, on my own opinion pitted against the rest of mankind . . . No—I'm sorry. But nothing would excuse me, in my own eyes—let alone the eyes of your mother and father—for taking you with me. You . . . you must stay behind. You will be needed here. I . . . I can't take you, Stubbins."

I felt crushed. It seemed as though there was nothing more to be said. And yet his final decision left me a little unsatisfied. When I had warned him of the dangers for himself in going to the moon he had argued one way, making light of the risk; and when I had asked to be allowed to come along, he had argued the other way and laid stress upon the dangers of the enterprise.

Resolving to make just one more try, I pointed this out to him and ended by saying, "If the flowers the moth brought, Doctor, grew on the Moon, there must be water there. Isn't that so?"

To my surprise he did not seem embarrassed by my stroke of logic at all.

"Probably, Stubbins, that is true. But do not forget that we are facing the problems and natural history of a life wholly unknown to us. The chemistry of these plants is something utterly new to our own science. That I know by pretty thorough investigation of them. To us the idea of producing plants without water is something quite impossible. But in the moon, again, who shall say? They may be air plants, parasites like our orchids, living on the moisture of the atmosphere. Or anything. No one can tell how they get their nourishment or carry on life till he has seen them growing in their native surroundings. Listen, Stubbins: If I had ever seen *a tree growing on the moon* I would feel I could answer your question better. But I haven't. And I have no idea whatever as yet from what source these flowers derive their life."

He paused a moment, then rose, and approaching my chair where I sat gloomily, scowling at the table with my head in my hands, he clutched my shoulder in a kindly grasp.

"Good friend," said he in a funny chokey sort of voice, "let's not discuss it anymore. You know, don't you, how much I'd love to have you. But I can't, Stubbins—I just can't take you."

· The Eleventh Chapter ·

OUR MIDNIGHT VISITORS

THE Doctor's answer to my request to let me accompany him had the opposite effect to that which he hoped for—or expected. I made no answer whatever to his decision that night. I went to bed. But there I lay awake thinking.

What might happen if I let him go alone? I recalled what Too-Too had said: "We, the animal members of his household, would be much happier if he had some other human with him." And then, I suppose, just the fact that my coming was forbidden made it seem all the more desirable and put me on my mettle.

Anyhow, after many hours of sleeplessness, I decided that I would say nothing, lie low, and remember Too-Too's advice about keeping a very close watch on John Dolittle's movements for the next few days.

And as it turned out, it was a good thing that I did so. It is the proudest thing that I can boast of that this determination, which the Doctor's refusal of my company bred in me, led to my eventually going with him.

From that night when I made up my mind I hardly let him out of my sight. No detective ever played a game of closer shadowing than I did. Whenever he sent me off on an errand I pretended to go, but sent Jip or Chee-Chee instead. From moment to moment I did not know when he might depart; but I knew where he was and exactly what he was doing. For I was quite determined that when he went he would *not* go without me.

In this, Too-Too was the only one who helped me. There were hours, of course, when I could not be on the watch myself. I had to sleep. At such times the little owl did duty for me. I don't think that the Doctor ever realized how closely shadowed he was.

The hour came at last. I was fast asleep. Too-Too woke me by gently pulling my hair. In a second I was wide awake.

"Tommy!" I heard. "Get up! Tommy! Tommy!"

"What is it?" I whispered. "What's happening?"

"Get your clothes on," whispered the owl. "The Doctor has gone out into the garden. He has his little black bag with him—and his overcoat. I have a feeling that things may be happening. Come down into the garden. Don't strike a light. Better be on the safe side. I can see. I'll guide you. But hurry—for goodness sake!"

My bedroom was so small and I knew the exact position of everything in it so well that it was no great feat for me to dress myself in the dark. I remember, as I felt for my clothes and finally drew them on, wondering what I had better take with me for this strange new voyage. What would one need most in the moon? Who could say? For who had been there? I had given this problem some thought already and decided that the freer we were of luggage the better. That had always been the Doctor's principle; and considering how impossible it was to make a choice in these circumstances, it seemed here a particularly good rule to follow.

My new big pocketknife? Yes, I must take that. I got it out of the bureau drawer. It, with a box of matches, was all the dunnage I took. Many a time afterwards I laughed at the solution. And yet, of course, I did not know for certain that night, as I hunched on my overcoat in the dark, whether or not I was leaving the house and the earth for the great voyage. Still, something told me that the little owl had probably guessed right. I could hear him fidgeting and muttering somewhere near the door, impatient for me to be going. He gave a grunt of relief when I finally felt my way toward him and whispered that I was ready.

Hopping down the pitch-black stairs ahead of me he led the way, by means of his funny little grunts for signals, to the kitchen. Here I very stealthily undid the bolts of the back door, which led into the garden.

I had not the vaguest notion what time it was. I knew Too-Too could tell me roughly, at all events, but I was afraid to call to him. The moon was visible, but only by fits and starts because the gentle wind was blowing clouds across the sky in a constant procession.

Too-Too waited a moment for me to get used to the dim light of the garden. He knew that my stumbling or stepping on a cracking twig might easily give us away. He whispered that he would go forward alone and reconnoiter. I saw him crouch for a spring as though he meant to take to his wings. Flying he could see more than walking and be less likely to be noticed himself.

But he did not leave the ground. Suddenly, sharply, he turned his head. Then he came back to me.

"Tommy!" he whispered. "There are strangers in the garden. Two men have just come in at the front gate."

As I bent down to listen to him, he hopped onto my knee, and from there to my shoulder, a favorite traveling place of his when we went about together. From this lookout he could easily whisper into my ear.

"Who do you reckon they are, Too-Too?" I asked.

"Goodness only knows," he replied. "We've got to keep a close watch on them, anyway. Then we'll soon know, I fancy. They're behaving mighty queerly—evidently anxious not to be seen."

"Do you think they might be burglars trying to get into the house?" I asked.

"Not the slightest chance of that," said the owl promptly. "No one in his senses would pick out the Doctor's establishment as a house to rob. Everybody knows he is almost always penniless. Everything in the house of real value John Dolittle has sold long ago. We must watch these birds and see what their game is. But it isn't plunder."

So, under whispered orders from the owl, I crept along in the shadow of bushes and hedges and tried to find out what our strange visitors had come for.

Very soon we saw it was a case of spying on spies. The two men, for the present, at all events, wanted nothing more than an opportunity to find out what the Doctor was doing. There was no question now that the secret of the giant moth's presence in our garden was out. His gigantic form, lit up by the moon's paling light, occupied the greater part of the back lawn. The black figure of the Doctor could be plainly seen scouting around it.

As a matter of fact, I found myself playing a double part and watching both the Doctor and the men. I very soon saw from John Dolittle's movements that Too-Too had guessed right and that tonight was the date that the Doctor had decided on for his departure. Several suspicious-looking packages lying about the lawn, besides the black bag, showed me that John Dolittle had made preparations of a more extensive kind than he usually did for his voyages. The question now that seemed most important was: Would these men try to interfere with his departure before he got away?

Altogether it was for me a strange and crazy night of adventure. At no time could I make up my mind whether it was more important to watch the Doctor than to keep my eye on the men. The men, I felt, were a menace, a danger, which at any moment might interfere with John Dolittle and with plans that could very possibly mean a great, great deal to the advancement of science and knowledge for the human race. On the other hand, if I neglected to watch the Doctor himself, he might quite possibly take flight with the moon moth and leave me behind.

While Too-Too and I were trying to make up our minds which we should give our best attention to, the men, to our great astonishment, came out from their concealment in the shrubbery and boldly walked up to the Doctor on the lawn.

"Good evening, Doctor Dolittle," we heard them say. "We represent *The Slopshire Courier.* We understand that you are interested in certain experiments and natural history research of a novel and sensational character. Would you be so good as to answer a few questions?"

"There you are—they're reporters!" whispered Too-Too.

"I had expected as much. I wonder how on earth they heard of the moth's being here though."

"Well—er—" the Doctor began, "this is a very unconventional hour for you to call on me. But perhaps, if you came back in a few hours—say, at ten or eleven in the morning—I might find time to give you an interview. Just now I am very busy."

The reporters who were clearly anxious to get the information they wanted right away (so as to be ahead of the other papers in their announcements) conversed together a moment before replying. Then they turned back to the Doctor. Neither Too-Too nor I heard exactly what they said. But whatever it was it seemed to be agreeable to the Doctor and in keeping with his wishes. For immediately after, the two men retired and the Doctor disappeared into another part of the garden.

It is quite certain that without Too-Too's aid in this night's work things could never have turned out as successfully as they did. I have often thought since that if the little owl had ever wanted to enter the profession of animal detective the great Kling could have been easily surpassed.

For Too-Too certainly had a gift for seeing things without being seen. Directly the men parted from the Doctor, he parted from me.

"Listen," said he before he left my shoulder, "I don't trust those gentlemen. We have a double job tonight. The Doctor should be the easier of the two because he will be less suspicious. You watch him. I'll keep an eye on the newspaper fellows. It may be that they'll clear out, as they said they would. And then again they may not. We can't afford to risk it. You go ahead and watch John Dolittle and I'll let you know if *The Slopshire Courier*'s men do anything out of the ordinary. Remember, whatever happens, the Doctor must *not* go on this voyage alone."

"All right, Too-Too," I said, "I'm ready for all emergencies. Go ahead."

With a little flirt of his wings, the owl left my shoulder and soared away into the darkness of the night. Then very, very stealthily and cautiously I made my way along the garden, keeping always in the shadow of hedges and shrubs, toward the great figure of the moon moth squatting on the lawn.

It wasn't easy work. For one thing I could not locate the Doctor himself for quite a while. And I was scared that any minute I might run into him and have to confess that I'd been spying. I didn't feel at all guilty about that. If Too-Too, speaking for the animal household in general, felt it necessary that he should be watched, I was very willing to do it without any qualms of conscience at all. What might not depend on my vigilance and skill? He must *not* go alone.

What was that? Yes, the Doctor's figure coming out from behind the shadow of the moth. In his hands he held two packages. I wished that I had Too-Too's trick of seeing clearly in the dark. Dare I move a little closer?

As a matter of fact I did not have a chance to, before I found Too-Too back on my shoulder. With a gentle fanning of wings he dropped down beside my right ear as gently as a butterfly landing on a leaf.

"They haven't gone, Tommy," he whispered. "Never had any intention to, I imagine. They clattered down the front steps, making a great noise, but almost immediately came back again on tiptoe. They are now hanging around the front garden close to the wall."

"What do you think we had better do?" I asked.

"Well, as far as I can see it's a choice of two things," said he. "Either we continue to watch them and see how much they find out; or we wake up Bumpo and get him to chuck them off the premises. Myself, I'm all for throwing them out. I think it can be done too without the Doctor's realizing that you've been watching him. That's important, of course."

"I think you are right," said I. "Suppose you take a spell at watching the Doctor while I go and wake Bumpo. I don't imagine they'll hang about long after he has recommended an early departure to them."

To this the owl agreed. And I wasted no time in getting to the business of rousing Bumpo—always a long job at best.

I found His Highness, the Crown Prince of the Jolliginki snoring away in the deadest sleep a fellow ever slept. By ten solid minutes of vigorous pummeling I managed finally to get a grunt out of him, and by keeping at the work without pity for another five I got him to sit up.

"Is it a conflagration, Tommy?" he asked sleepily rubbing his fists into his face. "It can't be time to get up yet. It's still dark."

"Listen, Bumpo!" said I, shaking him. "Pull yourself together. It's important, serious. I'm awfully sorry to disturb you, but it just couldn't be helped. Two men have come into the garden. They're newspaper reporters, it seems, spying on the Doctor. The Doctor himself is still working with the giant moth. We didn't want to disturb him. But these strangers must be gotten out, off the premises, you understand. You're the only one who can make them go. Get up and dress—quick."

PART FOUR

· The First Chapter ·
BUMPO CLEARS THE GARDEN

AFTER Bumpo had gotten really awake and I was able to make him fully understand what was wanted of him, he was not slow in coming to the rescue.

"Why, I never heard of such cheek!" said he as he climbed into his clothes. "What do they think the Doctor's home is, I'd like to know—a sort of general information bureau, open all night? Where was it you saw these miscreants last, Tommy?"

"Too-Too said he saw them down in the front garden, hiding in the shadow of the wall. But, listen, Bumpo: it is most terribly important that we don't raise a row. If you can grab them quietly and make them understand that they've got to go, that's what we want. We *can't* have a rumpus, you understand?"

"Of course I understand," said Bumpo, jerking on his coat and reaching for a club that stood in a corner by his bed. "They'll understand, too. Such cheek! I never heard anything like it. This, after all our watching! Well, well! Come with me. We'll soon make them shift along."

In the game of moving in the dark, of seeing without being seen, Bumpo was almost as good as Too-Too himself. Jungle training had brought him a gift that all his college education had not dulled. Ahead of me he went down the stairs, feeling his way without a light, till he reached the ground floor. There without hesitation he made his way to the front door, opened it, and passed out almost without sound. He signaled to me to hang back a few paces in the rear and then slipped across the gravel path to the wall.

In spite of his instructions I was not far behind him. I was pretty sure the Doctor could hardly hear us here unless we made a great lot of noise. Bumpo felt his way along the wall and presently, from the jump he gave, I knew he had met his quarry. Stealthily I moved a little nearer and in the dim light I could see he had the two men by the scruffs of their necks.

"Listen," he whispered in a curious, fierce hiss: "Get out of this garden as quick as possible and never come near it again. There's the gate. Go!"

Beside the two shadows near the wall his great bulk towered up like a giant. Not waiting for an answer he conducted or shoved them toward the head of the steps that led down to the road.

Here at the gate I saw, for the first time, the faces of our visitors by the light of a streetlamp. They certainly looked scared—for which they could hardly be blamed. To be grabbed unexpectedly from under a hedge by a man of Bumpo's size was enough to upset anyone.

They did not wait for any second orders to depart but bundled down the steps as fast as they could go, only too glad to escape with whole skins.

"He conducted them toward the head of the steps"

His job finished, the good Bumpo was immediately overcome with a desire to finish his night's sleep. I thanked him for his assistance and he at once returned to his room. As I wished him a very late good night I noticed that the dawn was beginning to show, a faint gray behind the poplar trees to the eastward. This, I felt, must mean that John Dolittle would either hurry up his departure before real daylight appeared or else give up the project till the following night. I wasted no further time in speculation but made my way, as quickly as I could without being heard or seen, around to the back lawn to find out what was happening.

I discovered the Doctor in a state of considerable excitement, conversing with the moth. He appeared to have made great advances in means of communication with the giant insect since I had last seen him so engaged. The apparatus he was now using was little more than a tuning fork. Indeed, it almost seemed as though he had found a way of speaking with his guest direct. When I first got a glimpse of him he had his head down close to that of the moth's and held his left hand on one of its antennae. Once in a while he would consult the tuning fork grasped in his right hand.

From the moth's movements, little jerks of the head and tremors of the legs, it looked as though he was busily engaged in getting some message to the Doctor. I guessed the argument was over whether the start should be made tonight or postponed on account of the approaching daylight. I crept nearer to the back end of the giant creature to be ready in case the decision were made for departure right away.

Of course in describing that whole night it is very hard to give a proper idea of the difficulties that beset me. The hour before dawn is generally supposed to be the darkest. Be that as it may, the moon certainly hung very low and the light was faint enough. I had no idea of how prepared the Doctor was. I knew from what I had seen, and from what Too-Too had told me, that he had moved certain baggage out into the back garden. But it was almost impossible to determine under the circumstances how far he had perfected his plans.

However after a few moments more of watching him, prepared at any moment to spring onto the moth's deep fur if he should make a move to fly, I decided that they had both given up the project for tonight. For presently I saw the Doctor's dim figure move away from the moth and conceal some packages beneath the shrubs. Also I got a vague impression that there was a hurried conversation between the Doctor and Polynesia, who appeared to be perched somewhere in the direction of a lilac bush.

As you can imagine, I was weary with the long watch and the excitement and everything. As soon as I saw the Doctor start toward the house I felt I was relieved from further need of watchfulness for the present at all events. Bleary-eyed for want of sleep, I waited till I heard the Doctor enter the house and lock the door. Then I made my way to a window that I knew was not latched, slid up the sash, and crawled in.

I knew my trusty lieutenant Too-Too was somewhere abroad still and that I could rely on him to let me know if any occasion should arise requiring my presence. My head had no sooner touched the pillow than I went off into a dead sleep.

My dreams, however, were soon disturbed by all manner of dreadful visions of myself and the Doctor flying through the air on the back of a dragon, landing on a moon made of green cheese and peopled by a giant race of beetles and other dreadful, fantastic insects, whose one ambition was to gobble us both up.

Again I was awakened by the good Too-Too.

"What is it now?" I asked. "Don't tell me the Doctor's gone!"

"No," said he. "He's asleep—for once in his life. Seeing how he has worked the last weeks, I wouldn't wonder if he didn't wake up for a fortnight. But we're having visitors some more. I don't know what to do about it. Those wretched newspaper men must have told the whole town. For all sorts of people are peering in at the garden gate. It is now about ten o'clock. And ever since daybreak children and nursemaids and every kind of folk have been hanging around as though they expected a balloon to go up or something. Bumpo, of course, is still dead to the world—he *would* be. And no one else is stirring but Dab-Dab and Chee-Chee. I think you ought to get down and take a look at things. It seems to me as though we'd have the whole town around us before long. And some of them are so cheeky! You never saw anything like it, coming into the garden and picking the flowers as though the place belonged to them."

"All right, Too-Too," said I. "I'll get up. You might go and see what you can do toward getting Bumpo underway, will you? It does take such an unconscionable time to get him around."

Too-Too, promising he would do what he could in that direction, left my room; and only half rested as I was—for it had been little more than five hours since I had gone to bed—I crawled out and started to dress.

Arriving downstairs I found that he had not exaggerated matters in the least. I peered through the study windows and saw that there was a large group of people gathered at the front gate. Most of them had not dared to come in. But there were a few bolder spirits who were already wandering about the front garden, peeping around the corners of the house, and whispering together as though they expected some strange performance to begin any minute.

While I was cudgeling my brains for some means of

"Peeping around the corners of the house"

dealing with the situation, Bumpo happily arrived on the scene.

"Don't let them think we're hiding anything, Bumpo," I said. "But they must be kept out of the back garden. The moth must not be disturbed or scared."

I must admit that Bumpo did very well. He began by herding out those who had strayed inside the gate. A few who were more obstinate he assisted by taking them by the coat collar or sleeve and showing them where the private premises left off and the public highway began. But for the most part he conducted the clearance with great tact and politeness.

It was quite evident, however, from the remarks of the people that the wretched newspaper men had blabbed their story in the town. Also, though they had not of course guessed the Doctor's destination, they had, it seemed, announced that he was about to take a voyage on the moth's back. This, of course, was natural, since they had seen John Dolittle preparing and gathering his baggage in the garden.

"When is he going to start?" the crowd asked. "Where is he going?" . . . "Will he really fly on the big moth?" . . . "Can't we see the creature?" . . . "Where are you keeping the animal?" etc., etc.

Bumpo, in his best Oxford manner, was very discreet and most courteous.

"Sh!" said he. "Doctor John Dolittle will make his own announcements to the press in due course. Meantime, be good enough to leave the premises. He is sleeping after many hours of heavy work and study. He cannot be disturbed."

A large fat man climbed over the wall beside the gate. Bumpo took two strides, pushed him gently but firmly in the face with his hand, and the man fell heavily to the roadway.

"It is not polite," said Bumpo, "to force your way into a gentleman's garden without invitation."

· The Second Chapter ·

THE MOUNTED POLICE

BUT our troubles by no means came to an end with clearing the garden of our inquisitive visitors.

Because they did not go away. They were surer than ever now that something extraordinary was going on. And while we had the right to forbid their trespass on the Doctor's premises we had no authority to prevent their gathering in the road. When I came downstairs there must have been about fifty persons. But when these had hung around the gate talking for about an hour their number was multiplied by ten.

The bigger the crowd became, the faster it seemed to grow. Every tradesman's errand boy, every carter going into town, every peddler—in fact every passerby, stopped and inquired what was the matter. Heaven knows what tales they were told. The Doctor's reputation was fantastic enough for anything already. It only needed a whisper that he was going to fly away on a moth to make any country yokel want to stop in expectation of a show.

John Dolittle himself had not yet woken up. I was in the

"Every tradesman's errand boy stopped and inquired"

deepest despair. The road was now jammed; and farm carts, carriages, and delivery wagons, utterly unable to pass, were lined up on either side of the crowd that thronged about the gate. Anyone coming down the Oxenthorpe Road now just had to stop whether he was interested or not, simply because he couldn't get by.

"Tell me, Too-Too," I said, "what on earth do you think we had better do? If this goes on we'll have to get some assistance from outside. I never saw anything like it."

"Look!" said he, peering out of the window beside me.

"Here come some police—mounted police, too. They'll soon clear the crowd away."

"I hope so," said I. "Two . . . no, three . . . four of them. It will keep them busy to get this mob scattered."

Well, the arrival of the police did clear the roadway, it is true. But that is all it did. So far as the people's interest was concerned, however, it made the situation worse rather than better. It was a little added excitement and sensation. The crowd obeyed orders and gathered on the pavements, leaving the roadway clear for carts and carriages to pass. But still it stayed.

Presently I saw one of the policemen come up to the foot of our steps. He dismounted, tied his horse to the lamppost, and started to ascend.

"You'd better go and see what he wants, Tommy," said Too-Too. "I suppose he'll ask what has caused the disturbance."

I went to the front door and opened it. The constable was very polite. He asked if I could tell him what had brought the crowd around and if there was anything I could do to make the throng go home.

For a moment I couldn't think of a thing to suggest. Finally Too-Too, who was sitting on my shoulder, whispered, "You'll have to wake the Doctor, Tommy. We've done all we can."

I asked the constable to come in and went upstairs to John Dolittle's room. I hated to wake him. He was sleeping like a log and I knew how much he needed his rest. Very gently I shook him by the shoulder.

"What is it, Stubbins?" he asked, opening his eyes.

"Doctor," said I, "I'm terribly sorry to disturb you. But

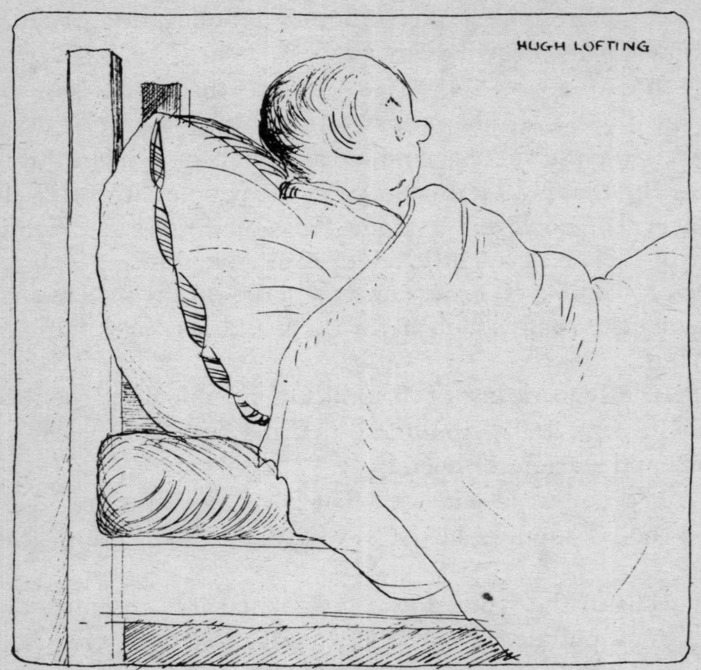

" 'What is it, Stubbins?' he asked"

we felt it just couldn't be helped. It seems that the moth's presence here has leaked out."

"Yes, I know," said he. "It can't be helped. These wretched newspaper fellows—you can't keep them out. Two of them came to see me in the garden last night."

"But the truth is," I said, "that they have blabbed their story to the whole of Puddleby, it seems. The road is just blocked by the crowd who have come to see you fly to the moon. The police have finally arrived on the scene, and they want to know if there is anything we can do to make the throng go home. They are quite polite. But we couldn't think of anything to suggest. So I came to ask you what you thought should be done."

The Doctor's handling of the situation was, I decided afterward, extraordinarily good.

"Well," he said, climbing out of bed with a yawn, "I suppose I must speak to the crowd. Just let me get my clothes on and I will see what I can do."

I left him and returned to Too-Too downstairs.

"Keep an eye on him," said the owl, when I had explained what had passed between us. "You see his hand has been forced, as it were. And—well—anything might happen now, you know, any moment."

I didn't quite understand what he meant. But I realized the need of keeping an eye on John Dolittle. I had no opportunity to ask the owl further what exactly he had in mind, because the Doctor at that moment came down fully dressed and interrupted our conversation.

After a few minutes' talk with the policeman he went out into the garden and, from the top of the steps, addressed the crowd in the road below. He began by giving them a general chatty sort of lecture on natural history, touching on various branches of study with which he had lately been occupied. This had the excellent effect of getting the crowd into a good humor and dismissed from their minds a good deal of their suspicions that he was keeping things from them. Presently he went on to explain that, unfortunately, he could not invite them in to see the garden and his collections just now, as he was particularly busy at the moment and things were not in order for public exhibition. They would realize, he said, that by blocking up the road and causing a disturbance they had—quite unintentionally, he felt sure—interrupted his work. If they would be so good as to retire peacefully, they would confer a great favor on him and the police. And possibly at some future date, if they would call again, arrangements could be made to show them over his establishment, in which they had shown so kind an interest.

To my great amazement the simple speech had precisely the right effect: The crowd actually seemed to realize for the first time that its behavior had been discourteous; and in almost an apologetic mood it at once began to break up and disperse.

"There's no doubt about it, Tommy," sighed Too-Too, as together we watched the throng fade away down the road, "they may call him a crank—but he's a great man."

· The Third Chapter ·

THE ERRAND

SO FOR the present we were relieved of *that* worry. But it was not very long after the crowd had gone that I almost wished it back again. The people, while they were a nuisance and one did not know what they might do if they continued to gather, were at all events a protection against something that both Too-Too and I greatly feared. And that was the Doctor's escaping alone with the moon moth. We felt that there was little danger of his making an attempt with all that mob present.

But when, shortly after lunchtime, John Dolittle came and asked me to go off on an errand for him to Oxenthorpe, which would keep me away from the house, I knew, till after nightfall, I got really alarmed. Stuttering and stammering, I made all the excuses I could possibly think of on the spur of the moment. I said I felt tired and asked could not Bumpo go in my place. But Bumpo, it seemed, had already been sent away on another errand. All my other efforts to get out of the trip failed likewise.

There was nothing to do but accept the job. But as soon as I parted from the Doctor I went and sought out Too-Too.

"Tommy," said he when I had explained matters, "you just can't go. That's all there is about it."

"But what am I to do?" I said. "I'm his assistant, after all. I can't refuse to obey orders."

"No," said the owl, putting his head on one side and winking a large eye knowingly. "You don't refuse—that would be most unwise—but you don't go. It is very simple. You just keep out of sight."

"But what can I say," I asked, "tomorrow, if he is still here, and asks me about the errand?"

"Tomorrow's tomorrow," said Too-Too. "And it can take care of itself. Even if he hasn't gone he's not going to kill you for disobeying orders. We can think up some excuse. But *don't go off the premises.* The fact that he is so urgent about this trip he is sending you on—and I don't know of any really pressing business he has had in Oxenthorpe for years—makes me suspicious. Also Bumpo's being already gotten rid of on some other job looks to me like clearing the decks for action. No, don't worry about tomorrow. By that time, if I guess correctly, John Dolittle will be on his way to the moon."

I finally decided the little owl was probably right. So with some excuse for reentering the back garden, I bade the Doctor good-bye and, with all appearances of dutifully obeying orders, started off down the road, presumably bound for the little inn about half a mile from our house, where the coaches stopped on the way from Puddleby to Oxenthorpe. But as soon as I was well out of sight I loitered about till the coach went rattling by. Then I made my way around to a narrow lane that skirted the Doctor's property at the back. There I scrambled up the wall and dropped down on the other side.

This part of John Dolittle's grounds was nearly all dense shrubbery. Of recent years he had found it hard, with all the studies that claimed his attention, to keep the whole of his garden in good order; and on this side there was an acre or two of tangled orchard and overgrown bushes that had been allowed to struggle and survive as best they could. It was excellent cover. Through it I noiselessly made my way till I was within a few yards of the back lawn and the tail of the moon moth himself.

And then began several hours of waiting. I was well concealed, and from behind some high laurels could see all that took place on the lawn. For a long time nothing seemed to happen at all, and I began to wonder if Too-Too had guessed wrong. Once in a while I'd see the Doctor's head through the windows of the house as he passed from one room to another. But finally, somewhere about half past six, when the sun had dropped well down to the horizon and a coolness in the air spoke of coming darkness, John Dolittle opened the back door and hurried out onto the lawn. With him were Chee-Chee, Polynesia, and Jip. As he came up to the side of the moth he was talking in a quick businesslike way to Jip.

"I'm sorry," he was saying. "I *can't* take you, Jip. Please don't ask me anymore. It takes so long to explain and I've only a few minutes. Remember those letters I've left on the study table. There's one for Stubbins, one for Bumpo, and one for Matthew. Show Stubbins where they are when he gets back and ask him to explain to everyone how sorry I am to rush away in this sudden sort of manner without saying good-bye. But I'm so afraid of those townsfolk and newspaper people coming back and stopping me if I don't get away now while I can. Stubbins will look after the zoo and Bumpo and Matthew everything else. Get those packages out from under the lilacs, Chee-Chee. And, Jip, you'd better go off and keep Gub-Gub amused while we slip away. I sent him down into the kitchen garden to dig up some radishes."

"Yes, Jip," put in Polynesia, "for goodness sake keep that wretched pig occupied. If he knows the Doctor is leaving for the moon he'll bawl the whole town around us in five minutes. What about the flowers, Doctor?"

"I've got them," I heard the Doctor whisper. "They're hidden behind the privet hedge. I'll get the packages up first, and then we'll attend to them. Where did I put that ladder? I wish Chee-Chee would hurry up. Keep an eye open, Polynesia, and let me know if you hear any sound."

The Doctor seemed much more upset about the possibility of being disturbed before he got away than he was over embarking on this perilous expedition. For me, my heart was thumping like a sledgehammer, for I realized that Too-Too had been right and there was every chance that the flight would be made immediately. With the greatest care, lest my movements be detected by the watchful Polynesia, I crept a foot or two nearer and measured with my eye how far I'd have to spring to get hold of the deep fur on the moth's tail. Once I had gotten a grip I felt I could easily manage to haul myself up his spine to the wider spaces of his back. These were now covered by his folded wings; but I knew that as soon as he took flight, provided I hang on at the takeoff, I could scramble up later.

Finding the ladder, the Doctor placed it against the great insect's right side and climbed a few rungs. Then he waited till Chee-Chee emerged from the lilacs with the packages in his arms. These John Dolittle took from him and stowed away somewhere up on the shoulders—though what method he used to fasten them by I could not see.

When this was done he came down and with Chee-Chee's help brought the big moon flowers out and stowed them away also. One, however, he laid down in front of the moth's head. This was grasped by the insect and drawn in close by his two front legs.

At length the Doctor descended again and took a final look around.

"Is there anything we've forgotten, Polynesia?" he whispered.

"You've left a light burning in the cellar," said the parrot.

"No matter," said the Doctor. "Stubbins or Bumpo will find it. Good! If we're all ready we'll go aboard. You follow me up, Chee-Chee, and we'll push the ladder down from the top."

· The Fourth Chapter ·

THE STOWAWAY

JOHN DOLITTLE wasted no time in sentimental farewells. It wasn't his way on ordinary earthly voyages; and one might be sure that his manner would be equally free from theatrical gestures when he was leaving for the moon. As soon as Chee-Chee had climbed up behind him he thrust the head of the ladder away with his hand and it fell gently into the shrubbery. That thrust was, as it were, the breaking of the last tie that bound him to the earth; yet he made it as though he were merely brushing off a crumb from his coat.

As the moth's wings began to lift I knew that the moment had come. The great creature was facing down the long sward of the lawn and he had some hundred yards to rise in before he would have to clear the willows at the south end. I was terribly anxious. I did not know this insect's particular flying form, whether he rose steeply or slantingly, suddenly or slowly. Yet I was terribly afraid of jumping too soon; for if the Doctor or Polynesia should see me I would certainly get put off. I must not be discovered before we were well on our way to the moon.

I finally ended by deciding that it was better to be too

soon than too late. If I should be caught and turned off, I might still stand a chance of persuading the Doctor to take me or of stowing away a second time. But if I jumped too late, then there was nothing to be said or done.

Luckily, both Chee-Chee and Polynesia started talking at the exact moment I hit upon to spring. This covered up what noise I made in leaving the laurels. I was in great fear, as I took hold of huge handsful of the moth's deep fur, that the insect would make some complaint to the Doctor—with whom, as far as I could make out, he had now established pretty complete conversational communication without the use of instruments or apparatus of any kind.

But my fears were unnecessary. I imagine the moth took my invasion of his fur coat as merely some more packing on of bundles. The hair was so deep that I found myself almost buried, as I drew closer to his body. This was a good thing because there was still a little twilight left; and had the Doctor or Polynesia come astern of their flying ship to make a final inspection, I need have no fear of being seen.

And so I clung, expecting every moment to feel my feet leave the ground.

I'm sure, on thinking over it afterwards, that not more than five seconds could have passed from the time that I grasped the moth's fury coat to the moment he started. But it felt like an hour.

I could just see the outline of the trees and the house roof against the darkening sky when those great wings beat the air for the first time. The draft was terrific and, despite the covering of deep fur in which I was half buried, my cap was torn off my head and sent flying into the laurel bushes behind. The rest of what happened was, for quite a while, entirely confused in my mind. The sensation of going up and up, the need to cling on in a very perilous position, the rush of the air as the moth gained speed—altogether the experience, for one who had never known it before, was bewildering, to say the least.

I remember vaguely hoping that the insect's hair was strong enough to hold my weight, as I saw we were over the willowtops, with a hundred feet to spare and still mounting, mounting! It required all my courage not to scramble up right away to the more level ground of the moth's back, where I could find the comforting company of the Doctor and Chee-Chee. I admit I felt very lonely back there when I realized we had actually left the world behind and the lights of Puddleby began to twinkle so far —oh, so far!—below me.

Up and up, and up! My head reeled when I looked down. So I decided it was better *not* to look down. We were in for it now, as the schoolboy says, and the most sensible thing was to make the best we could of the situation.

I shut my eyes tight and just held on. How long I remained so I can't say—probably about an hour. Then I began to feel cold. My hands were numb with clutching tense. Some part of my confused mind decided that this was the time for me to climb to the level of the moth's back, where I could lie down and rest. Glancing upward I saw that the big wings were beating the air well away from the moth's body. I need not fear that my ascent would interfere with the machinery of flight. I kicked my shoes off and let them fall thousands of feet—to the earth we had left. Then, grasping as best I could the moth's hairy body

"I kicked my shoes off and let them fall"

with hands and feet, I started. I must reach level lying soon or my strength would give out.

I suppose it was a good thing for me that I could not see the earth swimming and disappearing below me as I made that crazy climb. It didn't take so very long. But when later I did gaze down on the earth—a round ball with little lights stuck all over it—I realized that I might have been a great deal more scared than I had been.

I had not found either the Doctor or Chee-Chee yet. For the first few moments when I felt I didn't have to cling I

"Next to it Chee-Chee's skull stood out against the moonlit sky"

was quite satisfied to stretch myself out on this level part of the moth's back and just rest. Indeed I was sorely in need of repose. My arms and hands were so stiff from clutching that the muscles were numb and sore.

I was still somewhat unhappy about speaking to the Doctor. After all, I had deliberately disobeyed orders. Presently, when I rose and looked about me, I saw him. I made out first the shape of his high hat, surely the most absurd thing that mortal eyes ever met with in such circumstances. But I don't remember ever having caught a glimpse of anything that was more comforting and reassuring. It was pressed well down on his head and next to it Chee-Chee's skull, sharply apelike, stood out against the blue-green moonlit sky.

Yes, I admit I was very much afraid. You see, I had never disobeyed the Doctor before. It is true he was no stern disciplinarian. To me, as to everyone, he had always been the most easygoing, indulgent of employers.

But this was something new and different. In everything he had been the leader whose orders were obeyed without question. Here for the first time I had acted on my own in a matter of serious moment and importance. What would happen when he knew?

Very slowly I crept still farther forward through the moth's deep fur. Then, gently, I touched the Doctor on the shoulder. At the moment he was looking earthward through his telescope. He started violently as though some supernatural hand had grasped him.

"What? Who is it?" he asked, peering backward into the gloom behind.

· The Fifth Chapter ·

THE DOCTOR'S RECEPTION

"IT IS I, Doctor—Stubbins," I said. "I couldn't let you go alone. I got on at the last minute."

"Stubbins!" said he, lowering his telescope. "Stubbins! Why, I thought you were in Oxenthorpe."

"I didn't go, Doctor," I said shamefacedly. "I—well, I wanted to come for myself and I did feel that you shouldn't be allowed to make the trip all alone."

For a moment there was silence broken only by the steady hum of the moth's wings. I wondered what was coming, what he would say or do. Would he ask the moth to go back and land me on the earth? I noticed Chee-Chee's head turn and in the pale moonlight a sickly grin of pleasure spread over his scared face as he realized there was more company on this perilous trip.

"Well," said John Dolittle at length, and my heart sank at the cold, almost stern, ring in his voice that he had never so far used to me, "I don't quite see why you should begin now, Stubbins, to take it on yourself to worry about my safety and—er—disobey me."

" '*Stubbins!*' said he, lowering his telescope"

"I'm sorry," I said. "But . . ."

I stopped silent. After all, there wasn't anything more to be said. For a minute or two I sat wondering gloomily if this was the end of our relationship. It was, I had to admit, an enormously cheeky thing that I had done. I suppose, as a matter of fact, I might not have embarked on it without Too-Too's support.

But my anxious thoughts were agreeably interrupted. Suddenly in the gloom the Doctor's strong big hand gripped my arm in a friendly, comforting grasp.

"Just the same, Stubbins," I heard him say (and in the dark, without being able to see it, I could imagine the typical smile that accompanied his words), "I can't tell you how glad I am to have you with me. At the very moment when you touched me I was thinking how nice it would be if you were here. Heaven send us luck, Stubbins! Did you tell your parents you were coming?"

"No," said I. "I didn't have a chance. There was no time. Besides, I was so afraid that if I left the premises you'd slip away without me."

"Oh, well," said John Dolittle, "let's not borrow trouble. No doubt we'll worry through all right."

"You usually do, Doctor," said I. "I'm not afraid so long as you're with me."

He laughed.

"That's a pretty good reputation to have," said he. "I hope I deserve it. Look, you see that big patch of lights down there?"

"Yes."

"Well, that's London," he said. "And the white streak running away from it to the eastward is the river Thames. This bunch of lights over to the northwest is Oxford, I imagine. Look, you can see the moonlight reflected on the river all the way up from London. And that big white area is the sea, the Channel."

The map of the British Isles was, indeed, at this height almost completely revealed to us. It was a cloudless, windless night. And the moth's flight was steady, smooth, and undisturbed as his great wings purred their way upward, putting goodness only knows how may miles between us and Puddleby every minute.

Suddenly I realized that from being scared to death with

the newness of this situation I was, as usual with the Doctor's comfortable company, accepting the adventure with a calm, enjoyable interest. I found myself looking down on the world we had left behind and picking out geographical details as though I were merely gazing from a coach window.

He himself was like a child in his delight at the new experience. And he kept pointing to this and that and telling me what it was, as our great living flying machine lifted us farther and farther and made more and more of the globe visible.

But presently he panted and coughed.

"Air's getting thin, Stubbins," he said. "We are approaching the dead belt. Must be close on twenty thousand feet altitude up here. Let's get those flowers out and fasten them on. We've got one for all of us, luckily—five. Hulloa there, Polynesia! And Chee-Chee! The flowers! Remember what I told you. Keep your noses well into them. Come, Stubbins, we'll get them unstrapped."

As I moved in answer to the Doctor's summons I became conscious myself of how thin the air was. The least effort made me breathe heavily.

Somewhere amidships on the moth's body the flowers had been fastened down to a long belt that went about his middle. I joined the Doctor and Chee-Chee in their efforts to get the blossoms loose. The rush of wind made this difficult; and in the dim moonlight I realized that John Dolittle was asking the moth to slow his pace down till we had the work done. As far as I could make out, he did this by means of the creature's antennae. Those long whiskerlike arrangements were laid down flat along the back in flight and within easy reach.

"He did this by means of the creature's antennae"

It gave me a much greater feeling of security as I saw that the Doctor thus had his ship in control. It only took him a second to communicate his wishes to the insect. And then we hovered. The great wings still beat the air with giant strokes. But the ceasing of the rush of wind past one's ears told me that he was merely holding his position and, as it were, treading air.

"All right, Stubbins," said the Doctor, handing me one of the great blooms, "here's yours. Chee-Chee, you take this one. And we'll put this farther up toward the shoulders for

Polynesia. Now remember, everybody, life itself may depend on our keeping these within reach. If you have the least difficulty in breathing, take a deep sniff of the perfume. Later we'll probably have to keep our heads inside them altogether, when we reach the levels where there is no air at all. Is everybody ready? Get the flowers well down into the fur so they are not blown away when I give the order to go ahead."

In a moment or two Captain Dolittle was satisfied that his crew were prepared for the rest of the journey. And reaching for the antennae communication cord, he gave the order for full steam ahead.

Instantly the wings above us redoubled their speed, and the whistle of rushing air recommenced.

I found it not so easy now to look over the side, because I was afraid to leave my moon flower lest it be blown away. I gave up studying the map of the disappearing world and fell to watching the moon above and ahead of us.

· The Sixth Chapter ·

CROSSING THE DEAD BELT

THROUGHOUT I tried very hard to realize and remember every detail of that night's voyage. I knew the practical Doctor would never bother to remember those things that were not of scientific value to the world. Yet he and I were the only ones to see it who could write—though, as a matter of fact, both Chee-Chee and Polynesia remembered what they were able to see better than either of us.

Still, it was not easy. The moon moth put on his greatest speed when the Doctor gave the order to go ahead the second time. The noise, the rush of air past our ears, was positively terrific. It actually seemed to numb the senses and make it almost impossible to take in impressions at all.

But worse was to come. We finally reached those levels where there was no air at all. Then what happened is entirely confused in my mind and, for that matter, in the Doctor's, also. Moreover, no amount of questioning of the moth afterwards enlightened us on how he had performed the apparently impossible feat of crossing that dead belt, from where the air of the earth left off and the atmosphere of the moon began. I came to the conclusion at last that the giant insect did not himself know how the deed was done.

It is indeed no wonder that we, the passengers on this strange airship, saw and realized little enough of what was taking place during that phase. As we got farther and farther into the parts the Doctor had described as the dead belt, the moth's pace slackened till he was hardly moving at all. He kept working—in fact his great wings beat harder and faster—but the trouble was that there was nothing there for him to beat against. And soon the gravity of the earth itself, which was what he relied upon to maintain his position, seemed to grow fainter.

The result of this was that our flying ship seemed entirely to lose his sense of balance; and we, the passengers, all got desperately seasick. For hours, as far as I could make out, the great creature turned over and over, apparently helpless to get himself into any kind of position at all, utterly unable to go up, down, forward, or backward.

For our part, we were occupied with only one thing: and that was making sure we got enough oxygen into our lungs to go on breathing. We hardly dared now to bring our noses out of the flowers for more than a glimpse. There was very little to see, anyway. The moon appeared to have grown much larger; and the earth was just a tiny round pebble way, way off in space.

One curious thing was that we now had to make very little effort to stick on. It didn't seem to matter a great deal whether our heads or our heels were pointing to the earth. The force of the gravity was so faint it seemed you could stay clinging to the moth's fur as long as you did not actu-

"For hours and hours the great creature turned over and over, apparently helpless"

ally push yourself off. And even if you did that you felt you would merely move away a few yards into space and stay there.

We did not, however, you may be sure, try any experiments of this kind. We just sat tight, breathed in the perfume of the flowers, and hoped for the best. Never have I felt so ill and helpless in all my life. The sensation was something quite indescribable. It was as though gravity itself had been cut off and yet enough of it remaining to make you feel queer in your stomach every time you went around. Finally I just shut my eyes. My nose was bleeding like a running tap and there was a dreadful drumming in my ears.

How long we stayed wallowing there in space I have no idea. I felt as one sometimes does in bad weather at sea, as though the end of the world had come and that it didn't really matter, so long as it hurried up and got finished with the job. I wasn't interested in anything. I just wanted to die —and the sooner the better.

At last, after what appeared like eternities of this helpless, aimless turning and tossing, our craft seemed to calm itself somewhat and I opened my eyes. Withdrawing my head a little from the depths of the moon flower, I took a peep outside. I could not look long because the lack of air made that impossible. It was almost as though someone were holding his hand over your mouth and nose—a very curious sensation in the open. But before I ducked my head into the flower again, I had from that short survey of my surroundings drawn great comfort. I had seen that the positions of the earth and moon were now reversed. The world we had left was *over* our heads, and the moon, to which we were coming, was *beneath* us.

Of course this only meant that our moth had turned himself about and was headed toward the moon, instead of away from the earth. But, much more important than this, I realized that he now seemed steadied in his flight. And, while he still had only a poor atmosphere to work in, he was going forward and was no longer turning around helpless and out of control. As I popped my head back into the moon flower I congratulated myself that the worst stage of the journey was probably over and that very soon

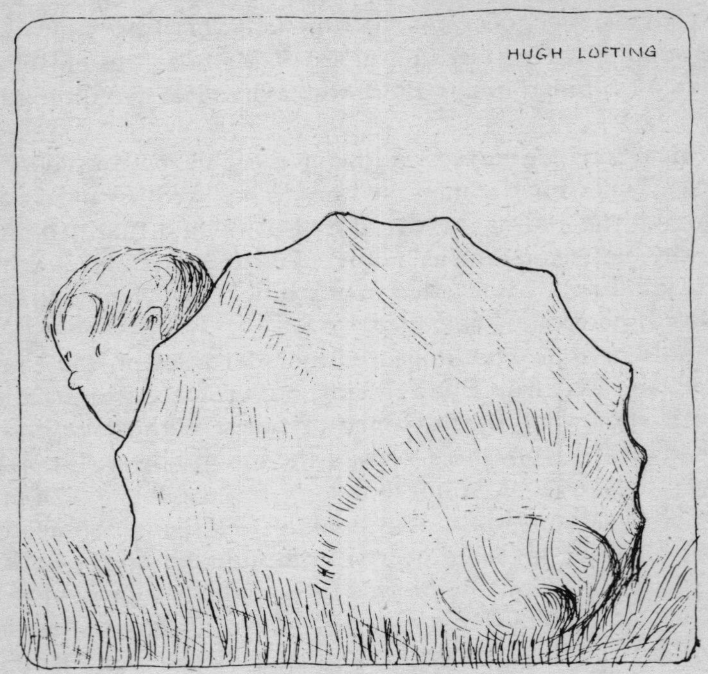

"I took a peep outside"

we should, for the first time in human experience, be able to feel and breathe the atmosphere of the moon world.

Also, with our ship once more in control and flying forward on a level keel, I suddenly found that I felt much better inside. I could open my eyes and think, without feeling that the end of all things was at hand. I wondered how the Doctor and Chee-Chee were getting on; but as yet, of course, I could not get into communication with them.

Little by little I felt the gravity of the moon asserting itself. At no time did it become nearly as strong as the earth's, which we had left. But you cannot imagine what a sensation of comfort it was to be held by gravity at all. That feeling—happily past—that you were tied to nothing; that there was no "up" and no "down" and no "sideways"; that if you got up too suddenly you might never get seated again, which we experienced going through the dead belt was, beyond all question, the most terrible experience I have ever known.

My sense of time on this expedition was just as completely destroyed as my sense of direction, and indeed of anything else. Later, when communication became easier, I asked the Doctor how long he thought we had taken over the trip. He told me that during the passage of the dead belt his watch had stopped. Gravity—or the lack of it, again—we supposed accounted for it. And that later when we got within the moon's influence and were steadily, if feebly, pulled toward her surface, his watch had started itself again. But how many hours it had remained without working, he could not say.

He told me that probably our best instrument for reckoning how long we had been on the voyage was our stomachs. Certainly we were both desperately hungry shortly after we had passed the dead belt. But since we had all been seasick for many hours, that is not to be wondered at; and it did not help us much in determining how long we had taken over the trip.

The Doctor also later went into long calculations about the light: when the earth was illumined by sunlight, when it grew dark; when the moon ceased to show sunlight and began to show earthlight, etc., etc. He covered pages and pages, calculating. But the fact remained that during the passage of that dreadful dead belt we had all been so ill and confused that no observations had been taken at all. The moon might have set and the sun risen and the earth both risen and set a dozen times, without any of our party knowing the difference. All we were sure of was that the Doctor's watch had stopped going as we passed beyond earthly gravity and recommenced when we came within lunar gravity.

Moreover, with the weaker strength of the lunar gravity, his watch probably went at an entirely new rate of speed after we left earthly influence. So, all in all, our calculations on the trip were not of much exact scientific value. Seasickness is a nasty thing.

From the time that I took that first glimpse out of my moon flower I began to keep a much more definite record of what was happening. As the moon air grew stronger I felt more and more myself. It wasn't the same as earth air. There was no question about that. It was much more—what should one call it?—"heady." This apparently was because it contained more oxygen than ours did.

I could see, as presently I grew bolder and took more frequent glimpses, that both John Dolittle and Chee-Chee were also picking up and generally taking notice. Polynesia, I found out afterwards, was the only one who had not been badly disturbed by the dead belt. Swirling in midair was, to her, as it was to all the flying creatures, mere child's play. If she had only been scientifically educated she could have told us how long we had taken over the trip. But the old parrot had always had a curious contempt for human science, maintaining that Man went to a whole lot of unnecessary trouble to calculate things that birds knew by common sense just as soon as they were born.

After a little, the Doctor and I began to exchange signals.

We did not yet attempt to leave our places as we still felt a bit unsteady on our legs. But, like seasick passengers in ships' deck chairs, we smiled encouragingly at one another and endeavored to show by gestures and signs that we thought the worst of the weather was over.

· The Seventh Chapter ·

THE TWO SIDES OF THE MOON

IN ONE of these passages of conversation between the Doctor and myself, I got the impression that he was making remarks about the quality of the moon air on which we were now being carried. There was no doubt that it was changing at an enormous rate. Finding anything outside my flower that I could breathe in at all, I was becoming quite adventurous and independent. I even went so far as to leave the flower entirely and walk, or crawl, down to where the Doctor squatted. But a violent attack of coughing just as I was about to say something to him made me beat a hasty retreat.

"Still," I said to myself as I dropped down with my head in my own blossom, "it is something to have gotten to him. Back there a little while ago I felt as though I could never see or get to anyone anymore."

Presently the Doctor paid me a flying visit. He too had to make it short. But we had the satisfaction of feeling that we were in contact. We had not been sure up to this that we could *hear* one another's voices in moon air. The Doctor had often spoken in Puddleby, when the voyage had first been contemplated, of a danger from this source.

"The ether," he had said, "is what carries sound with us here on the earth. We can by no means be sure that up there there will be any ether at all. If there isn't, ordinary speech will be impossible."

And with this in mind he had perfected between himself and Chee-Chee a kind of sign language. Too-Too had told me of this, and I had secretly watched their practice and gained some knowledge of the system.

So you can imagine how glad we were to find that up here also there was ether that could carry our voices. We found presently, however, that it carried them much more easily than it did on the earth. As we approached the moon and its new atmosphere became more apparent, we found that we had to speak lower and lower. It was very peculiar. Finally, if we did not want to break one another's eardrums we had to talk in the faintest whispers—which could be heard at quite a long distance.

Another very peculiar thing was the light. The Doctor and I had the longest arguments later on trying to settle whether we landed on the moon by earthlight or by sunlight. It would at first seem, of course, that there could be no question whatever on such a point. One would suppose that on the moon earthlight would be very little stronger than moonlight on the earth; while sunlight would be a hundred times as brilliant. But not at all. Something about the lunar atmosphere seemed to soften the sunlight down so that up there it appeared very little stronger than the light thrown by the earth. This had a very peculiar and definite effect upon colors.

Presently as the moon gravity became stronger, the

Doctor and I were able to get up from our lying positions. We still carried our flowers with us so that we could take a "whiff" every once in a while if we felt we needed it. But we could talk together in low tones and, in a fashion, make observations. It wasn't long after we thus "came to life" that John Dolittle asked the moth through his antennae communication cord to slow his pace down a little. We felt that it would be easier for us if we got used to this moon air slowly. It certainly had a very invigorating and exciting effect upon the human system.

Another point over which the Doctor and I argued a great deal afterward was, on which side of the moon did we land? The earth people have, as everyone knows, seen only one side of the moon. Maps and careful examinations have been made of that. Now, in spite of bringing with us the latest moon maps, it was not easy to decide on which side we were landing. Close to, the mountains looked very different from what they did through the telescope from the earth. *I* always maintained—and do still—that the moth deliberately went around to the far side before he attempted to make a landing. The Doctor swears he didn't.

How can I describe the last moments of that voyage? To say that I felt like Columbus first sighting a new world does not convey the idea at all. I must admit I was scared to death. And so, I know, was poor Chee-Chee. As for the Doctor and Polynesia, I can't say. I don't believe that hardened old adventurer of a parrot ever got a real scare in her life. With Polynesia, one always had the feeling that she dictated to Life, instead of having Life dictate to her. But that may have been partly due to her look of complete independence.

The Doctor? Well, I doubt if he was scared, either. He

had often told me that he had many times been mortally afraid in the course of his career. But I imagine it was never at moments such as this, when the lure of scientific discovery shut out every other feeling.

That he was thrilled, it is certain. Even the tough worldly-wise Polynesia admitted afterwards that *she* had the thrill of her life when the droning wings of the giant moth suddenly shut off their mighty beating and stiffened out flat, as we began to sail downward toward the surface of this new world that no earthly creature had set foot upon before.

· The Last Chapter ·

THE TREE

I MUST here speak again of this question of light. At no time, as I have said, was it very powerful. And one of its effects was to soften the colors in a very peculiar way. As we descended we found that the moon had a whole range of colors of its own that we had never seen on the earth. I cannot describe them because the human eye, being trained only to the colors of the earth, would have nothing to compare them with and no way of imagining them. The best I can do is to say that the landscape, as we slowly descended upon it, looked like some evening landscape done in pastels—with a tremendous variety of soft new tones, which became more and more visible the closer we got.

I think there can be no question that the Doctor and I were both more or less right in our argument about which side of the moon we landed on. In other words, we landed between the two. I know that looking backward as we came down I saw that both the earth and the sun were visible. The earth pale and dim in the heavens—as one sees the moon often by daylight—and the sun brighter but by no means as glaring as it appears when seen from the earth.

We were still at a great height from the surface. But already the roundness was beginning to fade out of the eye's grasp, and details were taking on greater importance. The Doctor, after again asking the moth to make the descent as slowly as he could, so that we should have a chance to grow gradually accustomed to the new air, had his telescope out and was very busy pointing to this crater and that mountain and the other plateau as features that were already known to us from the astronomers' moon maps.

From a certain height it was easy to see the night-and-day line, on our side of which the moon's surface was only dimly lit by the earth's pale light, and on the other more brilliantly illuminated by the rays of the sun.

Of course, I suppose anyone trying to land on the moon by mechanical means could quite easily have lost his senses and life itself in the attempt. But with a living airship that could accommodate itself to one's needs we had a tremendous advantage. For example, as we dropped lower and found the air more difficult to deal with, the Doctor again grasped the antennae communication cord and asked the moth to hover a few hours while we got accustomed to it. The great insect immediately responded to this demand and hung motionless in midair while we prepared ourselves for the final descent.

Captain Dolittle then called the roll of his crew and found that we were all at least alive and kicking—also terribly hungry. Sandwiches and drinks had been put aboard before we left. But these were long since used up. I have never felt so hungry in my life.

"The Doctor had his telescope out"

Over that last lap of the descent we took a long time. With the communication cord constantly in his hand, the Doctor approached the moon at his own pace. The night-and-day line moved, of course, very rapidly. Moreover, how much of that was confused with our own movement (we did not descend in a straight line, by any means) it is hard to say. This accounts largely for the difference of opinion between John Dolittle and myself as to which side of the surface we actually landed on. Close up, the details of all the moon maps no longer meant much. Because those details that we had seen through telescopes as mere fractions of an inch were now become mountains and continents.

I suppose the greatest anxiety in the minds of all of us was *water.* Would we find it on the moon? Moon creatures might exist without it; but we must perish if it was not there.

Lower and lower in circles slowly we sank. At first prospects looked very blue. The landscape, or moonscape, immediately beneath us was all, it seemed, volcanoes, old craters, and new craters—mile upon mile.

But toward that night-and-day line that showed around the globe we turned hopeful eyes.

I have seen the Doctor enthusiastic many times—when for example he discovered something new in any of his unnumbered branches of natural history research. But I never remember his getting so excited as he did when watching that ever-moving day-and-night line on our slow descent, he suddenly grabbed me by the shoulder. Forgetting for the moment how the moon atmosphere carried sound, he nearly deafened me with—

"Stubbins, look! A tree! You see that, way over there at the foot of the mountain? I'll swear it's a tree. And if it is, we're all right. It means water, Stubbins. *Water!* And we can manage to exist here. Water and *Life!*"

The End

· About the Author ·

HUGH LOFTING was born in Maidenhead, England, in 1886 and was educated at home with his brothers and sister until he was eight. He studied engineering in London and at the Massachusetts Institute of Technology. After his marriage in 1912 he settled in the United States.

During World War One he left his job as a civil engineer, was commissioned a lieutenant in the Irish Guards, and found that writing illustrated letters to his children eased the strain of war. "There seemed to be very little to write to youngsters from the front; the news was either too horrible or too dull. One thing that kept forcing itself more and more upon my attention was the very considerable part the animals were playing in the war. That was the beginning of an idea: an eccentric country physician with a bent for natural history and a great love of pets. . . ."

These letters became *The Story of Doctor Dolittle,* published in 1920. Children all over the world have read this book and the eleven that followed, for they have been translated into almost every language. *The Voyages of Doctor Dolittle* won the Newbery Medal in 1923. Drawing from the twelve *Doctor Dolittle* volumes, Hugh Lofting's sister-in-law, Olga Fricker, later compiled *Doctor Dolittle: A Treasury,* which was published by Dell in 1986 as a Yearling Classic.

Hugh Lofting died in 1947 at his home in Topanga, California.